St Elizabeth's Children's Hospital London

Dealing with sick kids can be heartbreaking, funny, and uplifting, often all at once!

This series takes a look at a hospital set up especially to deal with such children, peeping behind the scenes into almost all the departments and clinics, exploring the problems and solutions of various diseases, while watching the staff fall helplessly in love—with the kids and with each other.

Enjoy!

D1589675

Margaret Barker pursued a variety of interesting careers before she became a full-time author. Besides holding a BA degree in French and Linguistics, she is a Licentiate of the Royal Academy of Music, a State Registered Nurse and a qualified teacher. Happily married, she has two sons, a daughter, and an increasing number of grandchildren. She lives with her husband in a sixteenth-century thatched house near the East Anglian coast.

Recent titles by the same author:

*Moortown General Hospital

FAMILY
AFFAIRS

MARGARET BARKER

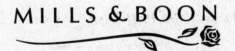

MILLS & BOON

All the characters in this book have no existence outside the imagination of the author, and have no relation whatsoever to anyone bearing the same name or names. They are not even distantly inspired by any individual known or unknown to the author, and all the incidents are pure invention.

First published in Great Britain 2000
Harlequin Mills & Boon Limited,
Eton House, 18-24 Paradise Road, Richmond, Surrey TW9 1SR

© Margaret Barker 2000

ISBN 0 263 82430 6

Set in Times Roman 10½ on 11½ pt.
112-0007-52866

Printed and bound in Spain
by Litografia Rosés S.A., Barcelona

CHAPTER ONE

As AMANDA hurried through the main entrance of St Elizabeth's Children's Hospital she could feel the warm sun streaming through the glassed-in area of the mini shopping mall. She always thought this section of the hospital was like a conservatory where it would be nice to sit by an open window, with the sunlight on her face, relaxing after breakfast with a second cup of coffee and the morning paper.

Especially today! It would be so easy if she weren't a career girl. She could stay in her own home and she wouldn't have to face a dreaded meeting with someone who'd had such a drastic influence on her life. If she hadn't met Edward all those years ago and he hadn't said—

She halted herself in mid-thought. That sort of reminiscence was soul-destroying. She wasn't going to dwell on the past. As her grandmother used to tell her, life was what you made of it. You made your own bed and you lay in it. What she didn't say was that sometimes the mattress started to feel a bit lumpy!

She smiled across at Mrs Lewis, the nicely plump, middle-aged lady in her clear plastic apron who was already selling flowers to a worried looking patient's relative even though it was barely eight-thirty in the morning. Mrs Lewis ran a hand over her blond, greying hair in its neat short perm and smiled back at Amanda.

'I've got the bluebells you wanted, Sister Grayson.'

'Thanks. You're an angel, Mrs Lewis. I'll pick them up on my way home this evening.'

What a treasure that woman was! Nothing was too much trouble. Tom needed some bluebells for a science project at school and Mrs Lewis had said she would bring some from her garden. Some of Tom's schoolfriends actually had gardens of their own, but as Amanda's London flat could only rise to a window-box the poor child had been a bit stuck. At the weekend she really must take him out to see real bluebells growing in the woods somewhere—if she could find the time.

She was now passing the small post office where Mr Goode was adjusting his gold-rimmed spectacles as he sold a stamp to one of the junior nurses who, by the grubby state of her uniform black trousers and white top, looked as if she'd just come off a tiring night duty. The pink epaulette on her left shoulder told Amanda that she was a student nurse, still in training, and therefore everybody's dogsbody! Ah, those were the days! She remembered them well.

At least, in Outpatients, she didn't have to contend with night duty. It had been out of the question because she had Tom to look after. During her nursing training, he'd had to stay in the upstairs flat with Alice and her little boy when the annual night-duty months had come around, but as soon as she had qualified she'd opted for Outpatients.

And three months ago, at the grand old age of thirty, she'd been appointed Sister in Charge of Outpatients. Incredible, whenever she had time to think about it! The responsibility had lain heavily for the first few weeks but she didn't think anyone had known about her anxieties and the occasional sleepless night because, over the turbulent years, she'd learned to keep her fears to herself. Everyone had their own problems to worry about.

But as she went in through the door of her office where the large print announcing her impressive title seemed to give everyone the idea that this was the place to come and complain when all else failed, she couldn't help but wish she didn't have the problem of the new consultant to contend with today. Out of all the men in the world, why had Edward Burrows been appointed Consultant in Charge of Outpatients?

She was barely through the door when, after a perfunctory tap, it was opened again to admit a smart, black-suited lady. Amanda felt a tremor of apprehension as she turned to face Mrs Imogen Drew, the hospital's principal nursing officer. She wasn't usually favoured with a visit so early in the working day.

'Sister Grayson, so glad you've arrived. I came along earlier hoping that you—'

'I'm usually in by eight but I had to take Tom to the swimming baths and—'

'He's here already!'

'Who's here?' Amanda had a sinking feeling she knew who Mrs Drew was talking about, but thought she'd delay the inevitable.

'Mr Burrows. I rescued him from outside your office only a few minutes ago and took him along to his consulting rooms. I've given him a cup of coffee and he's asked to be informed the minute you come in.'

Amanda swallowed hard. 'Why the great rush?'

The principal nursing officer smoothed the front of her pristine white shirt where it peeped out from the well-pressed lapels of her impeccable black suit. 'Mr Burrows is now Consultant in Charge of Outpatients, Sister. He fought off fierce competition to get this post.'

Mrs Drew lowered her voice in a conspiratorial fashion. 'I understand the interview panel were so keen to have him on the staff that they gave him a special contract. I don't know the details but, apparently, he'll be with us for a year and his schedule will include some work in

surgery. He's a skilled surgeon; an expert in kidney trans-
plants, I believe.'

Amanda smiled politely as she listened to Mrs Drew
singing Edward's praises. He'd certainly come a long way
since she'd first known him! But why, if he was a skilled
surgeon, did he want to be in charge of Outpatients?

'So you see it would be unwise to get on the wrong
side of a man who is so highly regarded by the powers
that be, Sister.'

Amanda went behind her desk and sank down onto the
swivel chair. Oh, she could easily get on the wrong side
of Edward Burrows! And the way she was now feeling,
after the morning scramble to get here, there was no time
like the present.

She picked up the phone. 'I'll give him a call. Thank
you, Mrs Drew.'

As Amanda watched the nursing officer's mouth set in
a thin line before she turned and went out, she reflected
that she wasn't going to stand any of this protocol nonsense. Mrs Drew was in her early fifties, a good twenty
years older than she was, and on occasions she'd tried to
pull rank. But Amanda was determined to run Outpatients
in the way she wanted to do. She'd made a few changes
since taking charge and she planned a few more, but she
didn't want to rush things—didn't want to be accused of
being too much of a new broom.

She loved her job but because of her home commit-
ments she had to be careful to use her time wisely. She'd
signed a contract stating that she would be on duty at nine
in the morning, but she was usually in by eight. In addition she stayed later in the evenings if there was a problem. What she would do without the blessed Alice she
simply didn't know!

She balanced the internal phone in the crook of her
neck. It was ringing at the other end. She held her breath.

For someone who was wanting to see her, he was certainly taking his time to answer!

'But he doesn't know it's me,' she said out loud, and realised that she was actually beginning to tremble. She was horribly nervous.

Twelve years rolled away whilst she waited and she was back home in her father's surgery, watching a young doctor seemingly throwing away his future career because—

'Edward Burrows.'

At the sound of his voice she came swiftly back to the present. My God! It really was him! But had he found out who she was?

She cleared her throat. 'Mr Burrows, this is Sister Grayson. You wanted to see me, so may I suggest you come along to my office in about ten minutes?'

'I'd prefer you to come along here, Sister.'

I'm sure you would! She had a million things to attend to but technically he was her superior so she'd better toe the line—for the moment! Kowtowing to superiors wasn't something she made a habit of.

Quietly she assented before putting down the phone and racing into her small, private cloakroom which was one of the perks of her job. After nipping into the tiny loo section, she re-emerged to wash her hands before staring at herself in the mirror as she raked a comb over the strands of auburn hair that surrounded her face. She had to admit that Michel had given her a good cut last weekend, but what a price she had to pay in his chic London salon!

Having her hair cut by an expert was one of the luxuries she'd given herself since taking on her new, exalted position. Even though she felt there were other ways she would prefer to spend her money, she knew she was expected to look smart and efficient and to present the right image.

She applied a quick dash of lipstick. The tinted foundation she'd rubbed in at the crack of dawn would have to do for the day because she'd left the jar back in the flat. Now that she had her own cloakroom and had to look presentable throughout the long day she really ought to duplicate her make-up and do some facial repairs after lunch. It was only the wicked financial outlay involved in two sets of cosmetics that was holding her back. Tom had been making noises about new training shoes and…

She made an effort to eliminate thoughts about her home life. Here at the hospital she had to give one hundred per cent. The new salary was a vast improvement and if she was careful she might even be able to start buying her own flat. She buttoned up her navy blue jacket and smoothed down her skirt. When she was in an administrative situation this was the uniform she wore, but when she was actually in a hands-on working situation involving patients she wore a white cotton top over a black skirt or trousers.

She always felt more comfortable in her working uniform but she definitely needed the boost of her power suit for this morning! At least until after she'd seen Edward Burrows.

Anyone would think she was going for an interview instead of just meeting up with an old acquaintance! She went back to her desk, turned on the computer and started to check the patients' appointments for the day. This was the time when she liked to concentrate wholeheartedly on her job. She felt like the captain of a ship, up on the bridge, ensuring that everything ran smoothly.

But concentration was evading her. She stood up and went over to the door. It was only a few strides to the consultant's door but she felt positively out of breath already. Realising that she was shallow breathing, she took a deep breath before knocking on his door.

'Come in!'

She opened the door and went in, closing it quietly behind her before she looked at the suave, debonair, handsome—in a rugby-playing sort of way—expensively suited man seated behind the desk. He'd changed, but not tremendously. She would have probably passed him in the street and then turned round trying to decide where she'd met him before. She would have wondered if he was a celebrity she'd seen on TV and then it would have all come rushing back as he'd turned on that self-assured, all-conquering smile as he was doing now.

He stood up and came round the desk, towering above her, his hand outstretched. She looked up and noticed a single grey strand snaking round the back of his ears, but apart from that he appeared very youthful for his age. She calculated he must be about thirty-seven now.

'So it really is you,' he said as he took hold of her hand. Almost as quickly he released it, as if remembering that he was trying to be professional. 'The name was the same, but I couldn't be sure it was you until you actually walked in. You haven't changed, Amanda. Apart from a few faint stripes on your forehead.'

She saw his full, sensual mouth relax into a wide grin as he said this and a surge of something akin to resentment flooded through her.

'I've earned those stripes,' she said quietly. 'They didn't just land there overnight.'

His brown eyes flickered. 'Tough, was it? Swimming against the tide is never easy.'

She took a step backwards. Her long legs meant that she was at least on a par with his chin, but she felt overpowered by his towering presence as she had done when she was a teenager. 'So, how do you know so much about me?'

'I don't. I'm merely guessing. I remember that conversation we had on the night before I left your father's practice. You seemed to be suffering from a severe case of claustrophobia.'

She found herself smiling at the memory. It was amazing how the passage of time could help her forget the agonisingly heightened emotions of youth when every day could seem like a lifetime if you were unsure where you were heading.

'A good diagnosis, if I may say so, Doctor.'

He smiled back at her. 'That's better! You looked so fierce when you walked in, I thought you'd turned into one of those power-mad sisters who like to terrorise the rest of the staff—especially new consultants. Would you like a coffee? Mrs Drew fixed me up with a large vacuum flask and some cups that would last me for the morning, or so she said. You can take it black or black.'

He had his back towards her now as he bent over the tray on his desk, but she could still feel the tension running between them. Had she really looked fierce when she came in?

'Black will be fine,' she said, accepting the cup and saucer he held out to her.

'Do sit down.'

She did as she was told, taking the chair at one side of the desk while he returned to his original place. They were being very formal again. What a contrast to the last time they'd met when she'd poured out her eighteen-year-old heart to him!

'So, I gather you gave up your place at medical school.' His tone was nonchalant but his eyes studied her face with the interest of an experienced doctor.

She raised her eyebrows. 'Who told you that?'

He shrugged. 'Well, that's what you were considering doing and as I now find you in the nursing profession it seems to me that you changed your mind about being a doctor.'

She took a sip of her coffee. It was terribly strong but she couldn't see anything on the tray that would dilute it. Her already taut nerves didn't need this extra caffeine jag! She put the cup down on the desk and leaned back against her chair, trying to remain calm.

'I seem to remember that you advised me to—'

'Oh, no! I didn't advise you to do anything. Whatever you decided was your own decision. I was merely the sounding-board for your teenage ramblings. You told me you were wondering whether you ought to go out into the big wild world and find yourself before you were launched into the same career as your father, mother, sister and grandfather.'

'And why did I start these so-called ramblings?' she said, her voice icily calm. 'Do you remember that, Mr Burrows?'

'It was a simple, innocent, meant-to-be-amusing remark. As I recall, I was talking to your father and he told me your place at medical school had been confirmed. You came in at that moment and I said something like, "So you're going to feed another daughter into the pipeline, sir," and for some reason you seemed to take exception to it.'

'Of course I did! It was very disturbing to a young girl to have her own misgivings stirred up by a twenty-five-year-old who was also contemplating making a vast change in his own life.'

Edward Burrows put his cup down on the desk and leaned forward. 'I'm not sure where this conversation is leading, Amanda, but I detect a great deal of resentment in your attitude and we're going to have to do something about that if we're going to work together.'

She drew in her breath. For a few seconds she didn't speak as the past washed over her like a tidal wave. When she did find her voice she spoke carefully and constructively.

'I'm sorry, Edward. I've been worrying about meeting up with you again, ever since I heard you'd been appointed.' She raised her eyes to his and saw something akin to raw pain in his expression.

He ran a hand through his thick dark hair. 'I can't think why. I was a trainee GP in your father's practice. I know he was furious when I decided that general practice wasn't for me.'

He stood up and walked over to the window, leaning his hands on the sill, his back towards her. Suddenly he swung round to face her, his eyes flashing.

'To be honest, I always found your father rather dictatorial. But I really cared what happened to his younger daughter, which was why I let you tell me your teenage problems. All about never having had a life of your own, always being expected to go into the family practice, worrying that you might never sample the real world and—'

'I know, I know. But you'd made a conscious decision to quit your GP training and go off to work as a doctor with a travel firm and I thought that travelling the world sounded such an exciting prospect, so…'

He moved back to his place behind the desk. 'You really did take our talk to heart, didn't you?' he said quietly. He picked up his empty coffee-cup, put it down, reached for the coffee flask and offered her another cup.

She shook her head. 'Couldn't drink the first one. It's pretty dire, isn't it? You'll have to come round to my office for a proper cup. I've got a coffee-making machine.'

He relaxed into a smile. 'Do I detect a waving of the proverbial olive branch?'

She smiled back. 'I wasn't aware we'd quarrelled.'

He threw back his head and laughed. The sound of his laughter did wonders for her tense nerves. She remembered how his laughter had so often resounded throughout the family practice and she'd seen the frown it had produced on her father's lips. Yes, he was right about her father being dictatorial. He'd mellowed somewhat since he'd retired and allowed her sister Yvonne to take over as head of the practice, but he still ruled the family with the same uncompromising attitude.

'Fine, so we didn't quarrel,' he said in an amused tone. 'We were simply clearing the air, were we?'

'There's a lot of air to clear, but—'

The phone was ringing. 'Excuse me a moment,' Edward said as he reached for the receiver. He listened for a couple of seconds before handing it over. 'It's for you.'

She smiled as she recognised Clive Goddard's voice at the other end. Their orthopaedic consultant had always been helpful since she'd taken over the reins in Outpatients.

'So this is where you're hiding. I've got a problem I'd like you to solve, Amanda.'

'Fire away, Clive. I'm all ears.'

She was aware that, across the other side of the desk, Edward was pretending not to listen in as he riffled through the morning post. She wondered if he approved of her easygoing manner when dealing with a staff problem. Her father would have reprimanded her, told her to keep her professional hat on at all times. Maybe that was why she liked to be as informal as possible.

And Clive was a friend as well as a colleague. They'd been out to the theatre a couple of times together and once he'd asked her out for a meal, but she'd had to turn him down because Tom had had a tummy bug and she hadn't wanted to leave him with Alice that evening.

'Sister Holdsworth's off sick again,' Clive Goddard informed her.

'Oh, poor Julia! That first three months can be hell if you suffer from morning sickness. I had an awful time. She'll be fine once the pregnancy becomes more established.'

She was aware that Edward's ears were positively twitching now! But she didn't care. She was surprised that no one had told him about her scandalous past. It was one of the first things that people usually revealed about her.

'Yes, well, never mind poor Julia tucked up in bed watching morning television while the rest of us soldier on. What are we going to do about it?'

'I'll come down and sort it out. Give me five minutes to change into my working uniform and I'll be with you.'

'You're wonderful, Amanda!'

She laughed. 'I know.'

Putting down the phone, she watched Edward look up from his mail with an innocent expression.

'Problems?'

'I've got to go and sort out a staffing problem in Orthopaedic Outpatients. I have the feeling I'll be there for most of the morning so...'

He frowned. 'But I'd hoped that the sister in charge of Outpatients would have time to show me round my new domain, introduce me to the staff, that sort of thing.'

She stood up. 'Well, give me an hour to help Clive Goddard and I'll make myself free. OK?'

He stood up and came round the desk, a smile playing on his full, sensuous lips. 'I don't think I'll be able to get used to this high-powered executive type you've turned into. Tell me, what does your husband think about your new job? He obviously goes along with it, otherwise you'd have changed your name and retired to some cosy little nest somewhere.'

He was holding open the door, looking down at her with an expression that she decided contained a certain amount of nostalgic fondness.

She cleared her throat. 'I'm not married. Look, I really must dash. Clive gets into such a tizz when his department isn't running smoothly.'

She didn't glance upwards to see the effect her answer had had on Edward. She couldn't blame him for earwigging on her conversation. She'd been sitting only on the other side of the desk from him, after all. He could hardly have put his hands over his ears! But to assume, as so many people did, that she had to be married because she'd had a child! She prided herself on the way she was coping as a one-parent family. Tom was a well-balanced, intelligent, happy ten-year-old who hadn't suffered at all from his unconventional upbringing.

'Am I glad to see you!' Clive Goddard said as Amanda, having changed into her working uniform, went into his consulting room.

'Where's Staff Nurse Broughton?' Amanda asked as she headed for the examination cubicle and began changing the crumpled sheet used by the last patient. 'She's scheduled to take over when Julia's not here.'

Amanda glanced over her shoulder as she sensed that Clive was watching her through the open door. From the crinkled state of his blue-striped shirt she could see that he still hadn't found anyone to do the ironing. It was two years since his wife had left him and his domestic arrangements were hopelessly inadequate.

As she turned back to smooth her hands over the examination couch, tucking in the corners of the sheet at the bottom, she reflected that, although he couldn't sort out his domestic arrangements, Clive was very positive about his social life. He was the sort of man who would enjoy your company for an evening at the theatre and expect nothing in return. Not even a goodnight kiss! And that was the sort of man she liked. No strings attached. As good as being with a girlfriend but with that certain frisson you could only get from the opposite sex.

Long may he stay that way! Because if he ever wanted anything more…

'Staff Nurse Broughton has been running between me and my registrar, but she goes at a fairly leisurely pace if you ask me.'

'Well, I'll stay with you for a while!' she said briskly. 'Quite like old times. Who's our next patient?'

She went over to Clive's desk and picked up the case notes on the top of the pile. 'David Shuttleworth, age seven.' Her voice softened. 'That's the dear little boy I took care of when he first had his accident, isn't it? I saw his name on the computer this morning. I was going to try and get along here to see him so I'm glad you called me in. How's he doing?'

Clive Goddard pushed a strand of fading, ginger-coloured hair out of his eyes and leaned back in his chair, beginning to relax now that Amanda had assumed control.

'He's a brave little soldier! It's his mum I worry about. She still hasn't come to terms with the fact that we had to amputate. She's still blaming herself for allowing him to play out in the street. It's a fairly quiet street and she wasn't to know that a lorry would try to take a short cut from the main road. She's always wishing she could turn the clock back.'

Amanda could feel a pricking at the back of her eyelids as she remembered the day that David had been brought in by helicopter to the heli-pad on the hospital roof. It was about a year ago, she remembered. She'd been deployed from her position as Sister in Orthopaedic Outpatients to help out in Accident and Emergency when the poor little injured boy had been carried in. She'd cut off the blood-stained jeans and found herself praying for a miracle when she'd seen the mangled left leg.

And that evening as she'd sat at the kitchen table with her own little boy she'd cuddled him against her, so thankful that he was healthy and uninjured. She remembered Tom asking her what was the matter and for a few seconds she'd been unable to reply as her mind had visualised the orthopaedic team bending over little David Shuttleworth, trying desperately to save his left leg.

In the morning, Clive had told her they'd had to amputate and she'd gone up to the ward to see David and tried to imagine how she would feel if that dear little boy was her own Tom. Wouldn't she be exactly the same as his grieving mother? Blaming herself. That was, after all, the nature of motherhood.

But you couldn't turn the clock back and it was a useless exercise to waste time on wishing you could. You could only go forward and make the best of what life had to offer at any given time.

'Are you OK, Amanda?'

Clive's voice brought her back to the present and she realised she'd been staring into space . 'Yes, I'm fine,' she said briskly. 'I'll bring David in.'

Her sadness vanished as she watched the plucky little boy walking into the consulting room, a broad smile on his face.

'Look, no crutches!' he said, leaning his small walking stick against the desk. 'And when I get my new pros-the...prosthingy...'

'Prosthesis, David,' his small, plump, anxious-looking mother prompted.

David grinned. 'Well, whatever it's called, when I get fitted with it, I'm going to walk without a stick and then...' he paused for maximum dramatic effect '...and then, I'm going to run.'

Janice Shuttleworth ran a hand through her grey hair as she slumped further down in her chair. She'd told Amanda at the time of the accident that she was forty-five years old when David, her only child, was born and he was the blessing she'd thought she'd never have. But she hadn't bargained for all the heartache. Looking at her now, Amanda thought she looked emotionally and physically exhausted.

'Would you like to take yourself off for a drink in the cafeteria, Mrs Shuttleworth, while Mr Goddard has a look at David?'

Mrs Shuttleworth brightened considerably. Amanda remembered that she didn't like looking on when David's stump was examined.

'Thank you, Sister. I could do with a few minutes to myself.'

Their little patient became even more talkative after his mother's departure, launching into a variety of subjects that interested him. There was still a sensitive area of the stump that Amanda had to dress. It was close to where the drainage tube had been inserted during the original operation, she remembered.

'Does that hurt, David?' she asked as she fixed the dressing in place.

The little boy smiled. 'No, that's great.'

Amanda put down her forceps and smiled back. She knew perfectly well that her little patient wouldn't admit to anything except intense pain. He'd been very stoical throughout the whole ordeal. He refused to feel sorry for himself and constantly looked forward to the next stage in his recuperation.

She patted his hand. 'You're a good boy, David.'

The little patient laughed. 'That's not what my mum says.' He was silent for a few seconds and his face became serious. Looking up at Amanda, he said, in a very quiet, almost inaudible voice, 'I'm going to be OK, aren't I, Sister? I mean, when I'm a man and everything and...'

The lump in Amanda's throat was so big she could hardly swallow it. That dear little face looking up at her was expecting her to be the fount of all wisdom. She who'd made such a hash of things!

But you pulled through, didn't you? The small voice of reason that always spoke when she was tempted to feel a bit down pulled her back from her negative thoughts.

'You're going to be fine, David.' She held his hand tightly and felt an answering squeeze. 'You're a fighter and that's the main thing. With an attitude like yours, you'll always pull through.'

'What's an attitude?'

She smiled as the tension in the air was relieved by the little boy's question. But before she could reply she heard a discreet cough. Glancing out, she saw Edward Burrows standing by the door.

'I did knock,' he said, in quiet apology. 'May I come in?'

Clive had been called away to another patient so there was no one in the consulting room.

'You can give me a hand, if you like,' she said. 'This is my young friend David and I was just about to explain the meaning of the word "attitude". Perhaps you could do that while I finish bandaging his leg. David, this doctor is called Mr Burrows and—'

'Why is he called Mr if he's a doctor?'

Edward was already inside the examination cubicle. He smiled down at the little boy. 'That's a good question, David. It's something of an anachronism, really, but—'

'What's an anachronism?'

Amanda's eyes met Edward's from the other side of the examination couch as she suppressed a smile. Rolling the tubular bandage over the dressing, she reached for the current prosthesis that she was going to fix back in place.

Edward sat down on the edge of the examination couch and looked down at David. 'The reason I'm called Mr is because I've specialised in surgery and—'

'Cutting people up and stuff?'

'Exactly! And that's what the barbers used to do in the old days. They were the first surgeons and they were different from the medical doctors—'

'Who didn't cut people up?'

'That's right. And the barbers were called Mister and we've kept the same title.'

Amanda tightened one of the straps on the prosthesis. 'Is that too tight, David?'

'No, that's fine.'

Amanda straightened out David's leg on the couch. 'Now, wouldn't you think they would have stopped calling surgeons Mister, David?'

The little boy grinned. 'Seems a bit past its sell-by date to me.'

'Exactly!' Edward flashed a grateful smile across the table at Amanda. 'That's what an anachronism is. Something that's out of place in the time it's happening in.'

As David sat up his face was a mask of concentration. 'But you haven't told me about that other word. What was it? Attitude?'

Edward smiled. 'That's usually to do with the way you look at situations. For instance…'

Amanda watched, intrigued, as Edward went over to the sink and poured out half a glass of water. Returning to the table, he held it up for David to examine.

'Now, tell me, David, would you say this glass is half full or half empty?'

The little boy's face was a mask of concentration before he answered. 'It's half full, of course.'

Edward patted his hand. 'Yes, it is. That's an example of having a good attitude and I knew you'd say that. People with a pessimistic attitude would say it was half empty.'

Amanda had heard footsteps crossing the outer room. Clive Goddard was standing in the doorway watching them.

'What's this, a philosophy lesson?'

Edward smiled. 'Something like that. When you get an intelligent young patient like David you've got to take time to answer all their questions.' He put down the glass on a small table and leaned towards the orthopaedic consultant, his hand outstretched.

'I'm Edward Burrows.'

'Clive Goddard.'

The two men shook hands. Amanda wondered if she was being hypersensitive, but she could feel a certain tension in the way Clive and Edward were watching each other warily. It wasn't going to be easy for Edward to take overall charge of Outpatients. The previous holder of the post had been in the hospital for years, retiring last month to improve his golf handicap. She knew that there had been a flood of applicants for his job from within the hospital and the fact that a rank outsider had been appointed hadn't been welcomed.

She busied herself with helping David off the couch, walking with him into the consulting room. His mother had just arrived back and settled herself in a chair near the desk.

'Mr Goddard will be with you in a moment.'

Amanda could hear Clive and Edward chatting quietly in the examination cubicle before they reappeared.

'Mr Burrows has persuaded me he needs a few minutes of your time, Sister,' Clive said, making his disapproval perfectly obvious. 'So, if you can't find me a replacement sister for today…'

'I'll be back in half an hour, Mr Goddard,' Amanda said quickly. 'In the meantime I'll ensure Staff Nurse Broughton is with you all the time and I'll redeploy another staff nurse for your registrar.'

She turned to say her goodbyes to her young patient and his mother, ignoring the large frown on Clive's face as she went in search of Staff Nurse Broughton.

'I can give you twenty-five minutes,' she told Edward, in a breathless voice, as she hurried along the corridor from Orthopaedic Outpatients. 'First, I'll take you to Ear Nose and Throat and then—'

'Amanda.' Edward's hand on her arm impelled her to stop short in her tracks. 'I'm quite happy to go round the departments by myself. I thought as Sister in Charge you would prefer to introduce me to your staff personally, but…'

'I'm sorry. I still haven't got used to all the time I have to spend on organising Outpatients. I sometimes wish I was simply a staff nurse, doing hands-on nursing and going home at night with no worries about administration and—'

He lifted his hand and put one finger under her chin, raising it so that she was forced to look up into his eyes.

'Well, thank goodness the crown has slipped!' he said softly. 'I was beginning to think I'd never see the real you again.'

He was smiling as he moved away, leaving her standing in the middle of the corridor wishing she could rewind the last few minutes on her life tape so that she could go with him round the departments to monitor the admiring glances he would get from her nursing staff.

Now, why on earth should she feel like that?

CHAPTER TWO

AMANDA closed one eye as she concentrated on looking through her auriscope into the outer ear of her tiny patient. The six final-year nursing students grouped around her in the ear nose and throat department leaned forward as if to put their collective eyes down the tube with her. Miss Jane Hartley, the smartly turned out, black-suited, grey-haired sister tutor, instructed her nurses to stand back.

'That's all right, Sister,' Amanda said, straightening up. 'I'm going to let them all have a look in a moment. You don't mind, do you, Jennifer, if these nurses look into your ear like I did?'

The little blonde three-year-old sitting on her lap smiled and said she didn't mind a bit. Amanda was thanking her lucky stars that the child she'd chosen for her demonstration was a model patient. In fact young Jennifer was the type of child who enjoyed being centre stage.

One of Amanda's responsibilities was to help the teaching staff with some hands-on nursing. She'd been told by a member of the panel who had appointed her as Sister in Charge of Outpatients that one of the reasons she'd been chosen for her new post was that she'd worked in every department of Outpatients and become skilled in the various techniques required. And since her appointment she'd been required to use many of these skills besides coping with the administrative tasks involved in her job.

She held out the auriscope to a young blonde nurse who had to be at least twenty to have got this far in her career but looked about fifteen. 'Would you like me to show you how to examine Jennifer's ear, Nurse?'

With Sister Tutor breathing down her neck, the poor girl could hardly say no!

Gently, Amanda guided the shaking hands towards the instrument and held it steady inside her young patient's ear.

'Wow, that's great!'

In her enthusiasm for the new vista the young nurse had forgotten her nervousness and become totally involved.

'Can you see the pearly white eardrum, Nurse?' Amanda asked.

'Yes, and I think I can see…' The young nurse hesitated.

'What can you see?'

As Amanda prompted her student there was a tap on the door. The sister tutor opened it to admit Edward Burrows.

For some unknown reason Amanda felt her colour heighten. Sitting there with a child on her lap and a bevy of nursing students clustered around her, she felt strangely vulnerable. But good manners prevailed. Ever since she'd failed to show Edward around Outpatients on his first day, over a month ago, she'd tried to remember that, although he might be an old acquaintance and her father's ex-trainee, he was now a very important man and she shouldn't underestimate the power of her new boss if she wanted to keep her own high-profile job.

'This is Mr Burrows, Nurses,' she said calmly. 'Those of you who are planning a career in Outpatients, after your finals, will see a lot of him because he's our consultant in charge of the whole of Outpatients.'

Edward smiled. 'No need to frighten them, Sister. I won't bite.'

A couple of nurses giggled, whilst the others gazed at the great man in awestricken silence and obvious admiration. Amanda had to admit that Edward cut an impressive figure in his brand-new, up-to-the-minute grey suit and highly polished, hand-crafted black leather shoes.

Did he stop off at the tube station on his way to work in the morning, she wondered, and instruct some enterprising young person to polish them until he could see his handsome face in them? All supposing he came in by tube, which was highly unlikely! Maybe he drove in from one of the posh houses that overlooked the park, leaving behind a delightful young wife and two point four children.

It was beginning to annoy her that in the weeks he'd been here she hadn't found out a thing about him. Neither had anyone else. According to the hospital grapevine, he was a complete enigma as far as his personal life was concerned. And nobody seemed to know where he'd sprung from before he'd claimed the top job that lots of the Lizzie's medical staff had been after.

'You don't mind if I watch, do you, Sister Grayson? I've got to make a report on current teaching methods in the hospital.'

'Be my guest.' She took a deep breath. 'In the first part of our lesson this afternoon I showed the nurses how to syringe an ear and then Accident and Emergency brought young Jennifer along.'

She bent over her young patient and smiled. 'Would you tell Mr Burrows what you did with your shiny new red beads, Jennifer?'

The little girl grinned mischievously, happy once again to be the centre of attention. 'I pulled out the string to count them and then I put one in my ear to see what it would feel like and it wouldn't come out, so Mummy brought me here and—'

'I could see the red bead against the eardrum, Sister,' the blonde student nurse interrupted excitedly.

'I'd like you all to have a look,' Amanda said. 'If that's all right with you, Jennifer. Are you comfy on my lap or would you like to sit…?'

The little patient twined her arms around Amanda's neck and said she wanted to stay right where she was.

The ear examinations completed by everyone, including Sister Tutor, Amanda picked up the long, slender, curved forceps and inserted them into her patient's outer ear to the exact spot where she'd seen the bead when looking down the auriscope. The ends of the forceps closed around it and she withdrew them complete with the bead. She felt a bit like a magician as she held up the offending object for everybody to see.

She saw Edward standing by the door, looking on in what she hoped was an approving manner. Over the past month it had become important to her that she gained his approval. Must be something to do with the fact that he was her boss, although she'd never allowed that sort of considerations to influence her before.

'Thank you, Sister,' Edward said over the hum of voices as the bead was passed round for inspection. 'If you have time before you go home, would you call in my office?'

She did a momentary check on everything she had to do at the end of the afternoon and decided it would be churlish to say she'd much rather see him in the morning. How could a cosseted man like Edward Burrows understand her complicated domestic arrangements?

'Of course, Mr Burrows,' she said, implying that there would be absolutely no problem.

One of the nurses had dropped the wretched bead and it had rolled under her desk. Sister Tutor was instructing a couple of nurses to find it and Amanda found herself ousted from her desk, standing up, clinging onto Jennifer who had suddenly decided she was tired of being a model patient and had started to cry.

'See you later,' Edward said, escaping the upheaval.

'My teaching sessions don't usually end in chaos,' Amanda said defensively as she sipped the coffee Edward had poured out for her.

He smiled, and, pushing back his chair, he rested his feet on a medical journal at the edge of his desk. He'd already loosened his tie, she noticed, and was looking more relaxed than when he'd hurried away from Ear Nose and Throat Department a couple of hours ago.

'I thought you coped admirably,' he told her, his face solemn. 'In my report I shall thoroughly recommend the Amanda Grayson Academy for the medical tuition of Young Ladies.'

She laughed. 'Don't go over the top, boss.'

She watched his expression warily. Was she being overfamiliar again? There was no way of knowing. And she was technically off duty. Glancing at her watch, she saw it was a quarter past six. Alice had to go out at seven tonight so Tom would have to be returned home. She hoped Edward would come to the point soon.

She took another sip of her coffee. 'Your coffee's improved since the first day you arrived.'

He laughed and the welcome sound helped her to relax as she leaned back against her chair.

'Couldn't have been worse, could it? That's why I got myself a coffee machine. Mrs Drew hinted that when I held consultations in here it didn't go with the image of the consultant in charge. Apparently, you're supposed to call for a handmaiden when you want a drink but I told her to…'

He paused and gave Amanda an uncharacteristically sheepish grin. 'Actually I didn't say anything, but I would have liked to. Women in authority can be very bossy when you're a new boy.'

She didn't know how to take this. 'Present company excepted, I hope.'

His long, slow-to-appear smile had the same effect on her as if she'd been waiting for the sun to rise from the depths of the ocean.

'Absolutely!'

His deep, husky tone sent a shiver of something akin to excitement down her spine. It held a kind of promise of things to come; shared experiences, perhaps?

Come on, girl! Get a grip on yourself!

She decided there and then that she hadn't been spending enough time with male friends recently. She was getting out of practice in the friendly banter that went on in totally platonic situations. She definitely needed to get out more, with the opposite sex, so if Clive Goddard asked her out for a meal in the near future she would accept his invitation and get in some more practice at having your cake and eating it. In other words, going out with a man, sharing the bill if he'd let you, and escaping with nothing more than an innocent goodnight kiss if you really found you couldn't avoid it.

But she realised, with a pang of resentment, that at this moment it wasn't Clive Goddard she wanted to practise with!

She leaned forward quickly. 'I'm afraid I'll have to go soon, so if we could discuss what it was you wanted to talk to me about I—'

'I was hoping you'd have supper with me.'

Ye gods! He'd been reading her thoughts! She swallowed hard before replying. 'You mean…'

His dark eyes flickered. 'Look, I know it's short notice, but I'd rather hoped we could go out this evening. There are so many questions I need to ask you—about work, that is. You trained in the nursing school here, apparently, so your knowledge of the hospital would be invaluable.'

Ah, so he'd been checking up on her! She noticed he'd removed his feet from the desk and was knotting his tie again. Even his voice had that professional, authoritarian ring to it. He was obviously making the point that this wouldn't be a social encounter. Well, as far as she was concerned, it wouldn't be any sort of encounter because it was completely out of the question.

She picked up her black leather medical equipment bag and fiddled with the metal clasp. 'I'm sorry—as you say, it's short notice and I'm tied up this evening.'

Tied up with a young son, his schoolfriend, a pile of ironing, an over-affectionate, demanding, attention-seeking cat and an inordinate desire for a long soak in the bath followed by an early night. Besides, if it was going to be a working supper it wouldn't count as research into the management of encounters with the opposite sex.

'Well, when you've had a look in your diary, we could make another appointment, perhaps.' His tone was light and dispassionate as he leaned back against his chair, pointing the tips of his long, slender fingers together.

She felt another flicker of excitement running down her spine. It might be work, but she would certainly enjoy going out with Edward—if only to bask in the glow of watching people admire her handsome escort. That was her main attraction to the proposition...wasn't it?

'Let me have a look,' she said, trying not to sound too thrilled at the prospect as she pulled her little black book from the side pocket of her medical bag. 'Mmm...' She tried to look as if she was rearranging her social calendar. 'Friday night's free.'

Alice never went out on Fridays. She was a creature of habit and always washed her hair and listened to music on Classic FM.

'Let's make it Friday, then,' Edward said, without even pretending to consult his diary. 'I know it's free. I haven't built up much of a social life since landing here.'

She smiled. 'You sound as if you landed from Mars.'

He laughed. 'Sometimes it feels like it. It's all so different in London, isn't it?'

She was intrigued. 'Different to what?'

'Different to all the places I've worked in,' he said quietly.

'Where did you work before you were here?'

He raised an eyebrow. 'How long have you got? I've done a lot of travelling since I was a raw recruit at your father's practice.'

She was dying to hear all about it but time was ticking away rapidly. She would have to tear herself away. 'I'd love to hear about it some time. I've also been around— as in travelling around,' she added quickly. 'But I really must go now.'

He moved swiftly round the desk and stood beside her. 'Can I give you a lift or did you come in by car today? I know you sometimes walk because I've seen you arriving in the mornings.'

Checking up on her again! She didn't know whether to be flattered or worried.

'I always walk. Couldn't cope with a car in London.' Even if she could afford one! 'It's kind of you to offer but I don't want to put you to any trouble and it's not far to my—'

'Nonsense! It's no trouble at all. I'd be delighted.' He was already taking her medical bag from her. 'That looks heavy. Let me walk along to your office with you and we'll pick up whatever it is you need to take home with you.'

'I need to change out of my—'

'I'll wait for you in the car,' he said hurriedly. 'They've

given me my own space in the underground car park in the first section.'

She smiled. 'In the posh section with all the consultants.'

He grinned boyishly. 'Exactly! Who would have thought I would ever reach such exalted heights?'

'Funny how things turn out,' she said almost to herself as she headed for the door.

He handed over her bag as she went into her office. 'I'll be five minutes,' she said. 'I'm the mistress of the quick change.'

In the cloakroom, stripping off her uniform, she had a sudden moment of panic as she remembered the state of the flat when she'd left it that morning. But she wasn't going to invite him in and it was unlikely he would climb up the drainpipe and peer in through the city-grimed windows of her first-floor establishment.

He was waiting for her in a small steel-grey, zippy-looking foreign number. She climbed in as he held open the door, trying to emulate the attractive models she'd seen on TV who seemed to be able to fold in their long legs without showing anything they shouldn't. Her right leg grazed the side of the racing gear lever.

'Sorry!' she said breathlessly.

He closed the passenger door and returned to his place behind the wheel. She enjoyed feeling the powerful thrust of the engine as they moved forward, like a racing car starting out on the first lap instead of driving up the curving underground track that led to the front of the hospital.

'Good night, Mr Burrows,' the porter said, giving a military-type, deferential salute as they drove past the entrance.

Amanda sank back against the soft, leather-cushioned seat. She could get used to this!

'You turn right at the traffic lights and then it's straight on for a few hundred yards…'

She continued her directions as Edward drove along the busy roads.

'I thought you said it wasn't far. Do you walk this distance every day?'

'Keeps me fit. We're nearly there. Turn in here and…ahrrgh!'

Her running commentary came to an abrupt end as the car narrowly missed two familiar young boys on roller blades, careering up and down the forecourt of the large building which housed her flat.

Edward ground to a halt. 'Are those boys allowed to—?'

'No, they're not! They're certainly not!' Her heart was beating rapidly as she tried to cope with the frightening thoughts of what might have been if Edward hadn't been such a skilled driver. 'I bought Tom some roller blades on the strict instruction that he should only use them in the park under adult supervision.'

She climbed out of the car, her maternal instinct to the fore. 'Tom, whatever do you think—?'

'Oh, hi, Mum. Mrs Freeman's looking after us because Alice had to go early to her choir practice and Mrs Freeman said we could—'

'I don't care what Mrs Freeman said! You know what I told you and—'

She stopped in mid-sentence as she felt Edward's arm stealing around her shoulder. It was a warm, strangely comforting arm that made her suddenly want to cry. It was so hard being mother and father to a growing child and the support of another adult was just what she needed at that moment.

A combination of weariness from her long day's work and anxiety about what could have happened if someone had driven into the forecourt and been unable to brake in time was reducing her to an uncharacteristically helpless creature.

Edward's hand tightened on her shoulder. 'Your mother's absolutely right, Tom. It's much too dangerous to roller blade here, right next to the main road. I only saw you at the last moment because your mother screamed.'

A small, white-haired lady had come to the main door to see what all the fuss was about.

'Oh, you're back, Amanda. Alice had to leave about ten minutes ago and the boys asked if they could play out here. I'm sorry if—'

'It's very kind of you to look after them,' Amanda said quickly, walking towards the main door.

Mrs Freeman was a kindly soul and she didn't want to upset her. She lived alone in a flat downstairs and enjoyed the company of younger people and, having plenty of time on her hands, she'd offered to help out whenever she could. Amanda had given her a key so that she could feed the cat if she was late home.

Amanda turned to look at Edward. Although he'd removed his protective arm, he was still following her, making it quite clear that he expected to be asked in.

'Do introduce me to your friend, Amanda,' Mrs Freeman said, smiling up at Edward.

'This is Mr Burrows, Mrs Freeman.'

The elderly lady held out her hand. 'Oh, I thought you looked like a doctor.'

Edward smiled. 'Actually I am a doctor but on the surgical side of the profession.'

'I see,' Mrs Freeman said vaguely. 'I was going to feed Fluffy, Amanda, but I couldn't find any cat-food tins in your cupboard and—'

Amanda stifled a four-letter expletive as she realised

she'd forgotten to buy that most essential item of food. Alice would have already stuffed Tom and Mark with toast and Marmite in her flat on the floor above Amanda's, so they could make do with whatever was in the fridge, but Fluffy would give them no peace until...

'I'll nip round to that supermarket we passed on the way,' Edward said.

'Oh, I couldn't possibly let you...'

But Edward was already behind the wheel again, leaning through the window and calling, 'Which floor, what number?'

Now, she could either stand outside and wait for the delivery of the cat food and wave Edward off, or she could go upstairs and transform her flat into the sort of place Edward would expect her to live in, encompassing the gracious ambience her mother had created at the Grayson family home. Only a miracle would do the latter, but she could hardly dismiss him in a perfunctory manner when he'd been so kind.

Her lips moved as if with a mind of their own and the die was cast. 'First floor, number seven.'

As she ran up the steps followed by the two somewhat subdued boys she was making a plan of action and hoping, uncharitably, that there would be a long queue at the supermarket checkout.

Wonder of wonders! A kind fairy had washed up the plates, mugs and cereal bowls she'd left on the draining-board in the kitchen. She turned to look at Tom and Mark who were settling themselves at the kitchen table, pulling pencil cases and exercise books from their satchels, obviously trying to get back in her good books.

'Who did the washing up?'

Tom gave his mother an angelic smile. 'Mark and me! Alice said she thought you'd be tired when you got back.'

Amanda would have liked to hug Tom but she knew it

would embarrass him in front of Mark. The two boys had
been brought up together since they were small and behaved like brothers, each sharing the other's mum when
their own mum wasn't there. Alice had moved in to her
flat upstairs just weeks before Amanda had arrived in hers.
They'd quickly made friends because they had both found
themselves in similar circumstances.

'Well, thanks very much. You've made my day!' she
told them, ruffling Tom's hair as she passed on her way
to the living room to pick up the newspapers and magazines that would have inevitably found their way on to
the floor. There was no time to dust, but she plumped the
cushions on the large sofa. Turning on the small lights
that sat on her side tables, she surveyed the room.

It didn't look too bad in the disappearing light of the
June evening. She'd rented the flat fully furnished when
she'd first arrived back in England nine years ago with
her one-year-old son. The high ceilings gave it an air of
grandeur which belied the worn but comfortable sofa and
armchairs. The wide, marble-surrounded fireplace was
never used, but she'd renewed the floral decoration in the
centre of the hearth only a couple of days ago when Mrs
Lewis who ran Dunwoody, the shop in the hospital shopping mall, had ordered too many carnations and given her
a large bunch.

The large earthenware vase she'd picked up for a song
in the Portobello Road looked good against the background of bullrushes she'd gathered. Acquiring the bullrushes had entailed Tom hanging out over the river, whilst
she, one eye on her precious son lest he fall into the water,
chopped through the thick stems that he pulled towards
her, on one of their weekend forays into the Essex countryside. Yes, the fireplace looked mildly dramatic.

Or so she hoped! She ran into the corridor and peeped
through into Tom's room, immediately closing her eyes

and the door on the chaos, whilst reminding herself that this wasn't a hospital management inspection. In her own room across the corridor from Tom's, she pulled herself up short.

There was no way she was going to allow Edward Burrows into her bedroom! Nevertheless, she hurriedly threw the white cotton-covered duvet over the mattress and pillows—just in case, as her mother used to say.

Just in case of what? Edward was the last person on earth she would ever...

She held her breath as she heard the unmistakable sound of Edward's laughter echoing from the kitchen area. Her brief respite was over. She would have to gather her wits together, behave like an adult with a responsible job and an almost-under-control domestic life.

She took a deep breath and headed for the kitchen. The scene that greeted her made her stand quite still in the doorway.

Edward was unwrapping numerous enticingly fragrant tin-foil boxes onto the middle of the kitchen table whilst Tom and Mark scurried around gathering up plates, forks, spoons and the chopsticks her Hong-Kong-based friend had sent her last Christmas.

'Fantastic!' Mark said, sinking down onto a chair and grabbing a plate. 'I love Chinese food.'

Tom subsided beside his friend. 'Me, too!' Looking up, he noticed his mother. 'Hi, Mum. Come and join us. Edward's got us a Chinese. Isn't that great? I'm starving!'

Her eyes met Edward's. 'Thanks very much but...'

He crossed the room and stood looking down at her with the sort of expression she simply couldn't fathom. Enigmatic, she supposed, finding herself overwhelmed by all sorts of emotions she couldn't cope with.

'I was starving as well, Amanda, so on my way into the supermarket I ordered a Chinese take-away. Hope you don't mind—but you did stand me up as my supper date, didn't you?' he added, with the sort of smile she decided would melt the ice at the North Pole.

'I only stood you up because, as you can see, I need plenty of time to consult my social diary. Life is just one round of glittering parties so you'd better give me fair warning next time.'

He put a finger under her chin and tilted her face upwards. 'You're a very special person, Amanda,' he said quietly.

She glanced at the boys and was relieved to see they were devouring their meal like mini-vultures.

'We'd better take our places at the table,' she said quickly. 'Otherwise there'll be nothing left and I'm starving too.'

The plates had been scoured, the boys had been persuaded to go to sleep in the bunk beds in Tom's room. Amanda and Edward were sitting either side of the fireplace listening to Amanda's favourite CDs. Rachmaninov's second piano concerto ended and Amanda gave a sigh.

Stretching her legs along the sofa, she leaned back against the cushions and gave a sigh of contentment. 'Thanks a lot, Edward, for the Chinese meal. How did you know we were hooked on Chinese food?'

He smiled. 'I guessed. Once you've travelled in the Far East—as I'm sure you have…' He paused and looked across at her enquiringly.

She laughed. 'Was that the cue for me to tell you the story of my life?'

He stood up and walked across the decidedly threadbare carpet to pour out the remains of the bottle of wine he'd brought with the meal.

'A little more lubrication to help with the details,' he said, with a wry grin. 'Tell me about your travels.'

She took a deep breath. 'As you said, earlier this evening, how long have you got?'

He stretched out in the ancient but comfy chair, putting his hands behind his head. 'I'm in no hurry.'

She noticed that he'd left his tie in the car, his shirt was unbuttoned to near navel, his dark hair ruffled to such a degree that he had a definite air of boyishism—if such a word existed! If it didn't, she would coin it now and capture the very essence of this highly attractive, charismatic man.

She'd never realised just how good-looking he was when he'd been a mere medical recruit, ministering to her father's every whim—or had she? Had she stifled the feelings she'd had for Edward because he'd been twenty-five, a qualified doctor, and she'd been eighteen, a raw schoolgirl planning to become a doctor herself, and then changing her mind?

'OK, I'll tell you about my travels if you'll tell me about yours,' she said, leaning back against the cushions and closing her eyes.

Immediately, she was back in those far-off days when her father had despaired of her because of her change of heart.

'You're ruining your future!' he'd told her. 'Yvonne's already passed her first-year exams at medical school. I'd always envisaged that the two of you would take over the family practice. I took over from your grandfather and your mother became a junior partner. Doesn't family tradition mean anything to you?'

In the intervening years, when she'd gone back to the family home and seen her sister Yvonne, now head of the practice, enjoying the cushioned lifestyle that was light years removed from her own status as black sheep of the family, she'd known her life would have been much easier if she'd given in to her father and followed in the family tradition.

She opened her eyes and looked across at Edward. 'I decided I couldn't go along with the family's wishes before I'd explored the world a bit. So I went out to central Africa as a voluntary worker in a famine area. I dispensed food and water, helped with supplies of medication, did simple medical tasks and some not so simple. When the medical staff discovered my parents were both doctors and I'd accompanied my mother on her rounds since the time I could walk, I was given more and more difficult tasks to perform.'

She leaned back against the cushions and closed her eyes again. 'I delivered babies on my own out in the bush, helped—and sometimes very much hindered!—by the relatives of the young mothers and—'

'So where did you meet Tom's father?'

Her tired mind registered the interest in Edward's voice. She hesitated. Where should she start? At the beginning, maybe?

'Mike was the doctor who brought me round from a very bad case of malaria,' she began quietly. 'He was the first person I saw when I came out of a two-day coma and I sort of latched onto him like a baby chick when it comes out of the egg and thinks the first moving creature it sees is its mother.'

Edward stirred in his chair. 'Are you trying to say you were deluded in some way?'

She stared up at the alabaster ceiling as the memories of the hot fever, the restless, sleepless nights under the mosquito net flooded back to her.

'I was certainly weakened,' she said carefully. 'But that was no excuse for falling in love with a rogue.'

He leaned forward. 'A real rogue as in…? I mean, are we talking criminal or…?'

'Well, he would have committed bigamy if I hadn't found out, three weeks before our proposed wedding, that he already had a wife in Australia.'

'Ah!'

A single, explosive sound, but Amanda felt that Edward had appreciated some of the trauma she'd suffered when Mike's friend had enlightened her.

'By this time I was two months pregnant.'

Edward stood up and crossed the space between them, sitting down on the sofa, one arm resting on the back, but near enough to reach down and hold her. She suddenly found herself hoping that he would do just that.

'That must have been—'

'It was!' she interrupted before his sympathetic tone could unleash the threatening tears.

'Did Mike stand by you?'

She drew in her breath. 'I didn't tell him I was pregnant because, at the time, he was being subjected to an investigation into the validity of his medical qualifications. In the event, he disappeared on the day that it was proved beyond doubt that he was totally unqualified.'

'Have you seen him since then?' His arm crept along the back of the sofa and rested on her shoulders. She felt a comforting squeeze and looked up into his dark brown, expressively sympathetic eyes.

'No.' She hesitated. 'Two years after I started my nursing training at St Elizabeth's I got a letter from one of my ex-colleagues in Africa. They told me that Mike had been killed in a car crash in Australia, soon after he'd gone back to his wife.'

'You've had a hard time,' Edward said gently as he pulled her towards him.

She leaned her head against his shoulder, revelling in the male scent of his aftershave. She could drown herself in sharing her experiences like this! Even recounting the traumas she'd been through wasn't difficult when she was sharing it with someone as understanding as Edward.

Was he so understanding because he'd also suffered in the intervening years?

'And what about you?' she asked quickly. 'Where did you travel to after you left Dad's practice?'

She watched the enigmatic smile spread across his lips. 'Shall we leave that till episode two of the Burrows/Grayson saga? You look as if you'll fall asleep before I get started on chapter one.'

She opened her hazel eyes wide. 'I'm really not tired. I…'

He pulled her against him and, without warning, brought his lips down against hers. She stifled the sigh that threatened to escape her own lips as she capitulated to his deepening kiss. Seconds later he was pulling himself away, his eyes searching her face for some reaction as if fearing she might object.

Object! It was the most exciting experience that had happened to her since…she couldn't remember when. Had she ever felt like that since those misguided days when she'd allowed herself to be swept along by the demands of an older, worldly experienced man; those days when she'd mistaken gratitude to the man she believed had saved her life for love?

'The one good thing that came out of my drastic liaison with Mike was my wonderful son, Tom,' she said quietly, almost to herself.

'He's a fantastic boy,' Edward said. 'You must be very proud of him.'

'I am.'

He was standing up. If she was more experienced in these matters she would ask him to stay longer, go out to the kitchen, delay him with coffee, brandy—if she had some—anything not to break up the warm—dare she say exciting?—rapport that had built up between them.

'See you in the morning, Amanda.' He was holding out his hand towards her.

She allowed herself to be hauled to her feet, hoping he would pull her against him and kiss her again...but he didn't. Again, she wished she were more experienced. She might have travelled the world but she was still ignorant of the uncharted waters of the heart.

And her heart was certainly beating much faster than it should be!

She followed him to the door. 'Goodnight, Edward.'

He turned. 'Thanks for—'

'I should be thanking you for the supper—and the transport home.'

Fluffy chose that moment to curl herself round Amanda's legs and break into a loud purring noise that reverberated up to the high ceiling.

'And Fluffy's saying thank you for the cat food,' she said.

He leaned forward and brushed his lips near the side of her cheek rather in the way people did after an impersonal dinner party. He didn't exactly say, 'Mwahh!' but it wasn't in any way sexy. It was the sort of non-tactile kiss you gave to colleagues who'd allowed you to spend the evening in the bosom of their family.

How did she get him to move on from here? But did she want their relationship to progress any further?

She tried to tell herself she didn't. Her romantic feelings had been brought on by the bottle of wine they'd shared between them, and his amazingly sympathetic manner...and the fact that as he stood in front of her now he was looking drop-dead gorgeous and if only she knew how to cope with seduction she would...

'See you tomorrow, Amanda,' he said amicably as the door closed behind him.

CHAPTER THREE

AMANDA carefully cut through the plaster of Paris with the special saw and eased the hard casing off the little boy's arm.

'Are you OK, Timmy?' she asked her five-year-old patient.

His eyes were closed so there was no way of knowing how he felt and he seemed to be gritting his teeth. He opened his eyes and nodded, but the mischievous grin was still absent. It was two weeks since he'd broken the ulna bone in his right arm but a fall in the school playground that morning was the reason he was having another X-ray and a change of plaster.

The radiographer was waiting for them and helped Amanda to place the little arm in the correct position.

'Don't leave me, will you, Sister?' Timmy said, clinging onto her with his good arm.

Amanda squeezed his hand. 'Of course not, Timmy. And when we've checked the X-ray photos of your arm I'll put it back in a nice new plaster and—'

'Can I keep the old plaster? It's got loads of names on it.'

'Keep quite still now, Timmy,' the radiographer said.

'Of course you can keep the old plaster, Timmy. I'll wrap it up for you as soon as we've got the other one back in place.'

She was aware that someone had come into the room. Turning quickly, she saw Edward.

'I heard you were working in Orthopaedics again,' he said. 'Julia still taking time off?'

Amanda nodded, her eyes back on the patient. 'I'm afraid so.'

'We'll have to replace her if this continues.'

'It's the early part of her pregnancy,' Amanda said quickly.

She knew how desperately Julia needed to keep her salary for the new baby. Her husband had recently been made redundant so Julia was the breadwinner until he could get another job.

Timmy stirred on the X-ray table. 'How much longer, Sister?'

'Nearly finished, Timmy. We're just checking your photos.'

The radiographer was returning from the outer room, smiling and nodding. 'No further damage, I'm pleased to say, Timmy.'

Timmy's customary cheeky grin returned. 'Great! So can I go now?'

'As soon as I've put the new plaster on you,' Amanda said.

Edward leaned over the little boy. 'What happened to you, Timmy?'

Timmy's grin expanded. 'First or second time?'

'Oh, I see. This is a repeat performance, is it?' Edward said solemnly. 'Well, you'd better start at the beginning. Will you tell me all about it while Sister puts your new plaster on?'

Having Edward watching whilst she spread the plaster bandages over Timmy's arm made her nervous at first, but he proved to be so helpful in entertaining their little patient that she soon got into her normal stride. And Timmy's bright chatter was always amusing.

'So, let me get this straight, Timmy,' Edward said as soon as he could interrupt the non-stop monologue. 'You fell off your bike the first time and this morning you came off your roller blades in the playground.'

Timmy pulled a face. 'I wouldn't have fallen this morning if I hadn't had my arm in plaster. It puts me off my balance.'

Edward glanced at Amanda across the other side of the treatment table. 'I can imagine it would. Don't you think it might be better to give up the roller blades until your arm's out of plaster?'

The little boy looked horrified. 'I've got to practise, you know. And this plaster's going to be on for ages, isn't it, Sister?'

She gave her patient a wry smile. 'Only another three weeks, Timmy. So, maybe you should hang up your blades until after the plaster comes off.'

Timmy's eyes widened as he stared up at Amanda. 'Do you really think so?'

She nodded. 'Yes, I do.'

The little boy shrugged. 'OK, then. If you say so.'

Amanda was adjusting the plaster, trimming the ends with her scissors. 'Will you move your fingers for me, Timmy? That's right...good boy. I'll take you to find Mummy now.'

'Before you go, Sister,' Edward said as they reached the door, 'you haven't forgotten it's Friday, have you?'

She felt an embarrassing heightening of colour spreading over her cheeks. 'Of course not.'

She certainly hadn't forgotten it was Friday! She'd been so relieved, on the day after their Chinese meal at home, when Edward had called her into his office, thanked her for his enjoyable evening and asked if she was still free on Friday for the working dinner he'd planned. He'd picked up the phone there and then and made the restaurant reservation. If she hadn't been so busy all day, she would have been worrying about what to wear tonight.

Edward followed her out into the waiting area . As soon as Timmy had been reunited with his mother, Amanda said she'd have to go back to Clive Goddard's consulting room to check that he didn't need her any more.

'I'll come with you,' Edward said quickly. 'I want to discuss the staffing situation with Clive. I think maybe we'd better get a replacement sister in Orthopaedics full-time.'

He held open the door to the orthopaedic consultant's room and she went in, feeling apprehensive about the outcome of a discussion between Clive and Edward. Julia Holdsworth had been an efficient sister before she'd become pregnant but her work record since then had been poor.

As she listened to the two consultants discussing the situation her heart sank. It was so difficult to be professional in these situations. But she had to say something in Julia's defence.

'I think Julia won't need time off as soon as the pregnancy becomes established,' she said. 'If you could just give her another couple of weeks...'

'You're very loyal, Amanda,' Clive said. 'But you can't let your sympathies get in the way of running an efficient department.'

Edward was nodding. 'I agree. I'll arrange for a nursing agency sister to be redeployed for the duration of Julia's pregnancy and the first few weeks after the baby is born. That way, Julia won't lose out on her salary, which I know is what Amanda was worrying about, wasn't it?'

She flashed him a grateful smile. 'Reading my mind again?'

He smiled back. 'Sometimes you're positively transparent.'

Amanda was aware that Clive was watching them, a curious expression on his face.

'Well, you two seem to be working well together in running Outpatients,' he said in a carefully controlled tone of voice.

Edward smiled. 'Yes, I think you could say we managed to sort out our differences of opinion in an amicable fashion. We haven't always seen eye to eye during the first month I've been here but our working relationship is improving.'

'It's all about communication, isn't it?' Clive said quietly, swivelling around in his chair so that he could study them both as they sat together in the seats usually occupied by the patients' relatives.

Edward seemed to warm to the subject. 'Oh, absolutely! In fact, I've arranged to take Amanda out for dinner tonight so that we can sort out a few problems over a working meal.'

Clive's green eyes flickered. 'Have you, indeed? Going anywhere nice?'

Amanda could feel the tension as Edward named the well-known, decidedly upmarket London restaurant.

Clive tapped a pen against his teeth, which Amanda had noticed he always did when he was annoyed or worried about something. 'Bit pricey for a working dinner, I would have thought.'

'Not a bit of it. I can't take our sister in charge to a cheap place, now, can I?'

Amanda stepped in to try to diffuse the tense atmosphere. 'The implication being that I'm only used to meals in posh restaurants, I suppose, whereas I would be perfectly happy with—'

'I'm sure you would,' Clive cut in evenly. 'But I expect Edward has other plans and I'm sure he'll be claiming expenses so—'

'You must be joking!' Edward raised both eyebrows as he concentrated all his attention on Clive. 'It may be a working dinner but I can hardly call it a duty if Amanda is with me so—'

The phone was ringing. Clive gave a curt, 'Excuse me,' before answering it. His face clouded over for a few seconds before he cupped his hand over the receiver and faced Amanda and Edward.

'It's Tim Robertson, Consultant in Charge of Accident and Emergency. He wants to speak to Mr Burrows or Sister Grayson, neither of whom is in their office, he tells me,' he said quietly.

'I'll take it,' Edward said evenly.

Amanda watched as the expression on his face became more and more worried. She was relieved when he turned to enlighten her.

'There's an emergency situation in Accident and Emergency. A school coach has crashed on the outskirts of London and they're bringing in the casualties. Attending to the newly arrived emergency patients means there's a backlog of patients in the waiting room. Tim wants to know if they can send some patients along here—'

'But it's almost six o'clock,' Clive interrupted. 'Most of the outpatient staff have worked a full day and—'

'It's an emergency,' Edward said. 'No one is obliged to stay but if—'

'Tell him to start sending the patients,' Amanda put in quickly. 'I'll go round the departments and round up as many staff as possible.'

'Thanks.' Edward spoke again briefly into the phone before replacing it on Clive's desk. 'You're not obliged to stay, Clive, but there are a number of orthopaedic casualties, as you can imagine, and—'

'Of course I'll stay,' Clive said curtly. 'And I'll keep on as many of the staff as I can.'

Amanda, going out of the door to round up the willing

helpers, felt a certain sense of relief that Clive and Edward had come to an agreement on something. What was it with these two that they seemed to find the need to wind each other up?

She had no time to dwell on the problem during the next three hours. It was all hands on deck as they dealt with traumatised children who'd been thrown from their seats as the school coach had collided with a lorry. Amazingly, there were no fatalities, but there were some seriously injured little patients.

She was kept busy moving between X-ray and the plaster room, fixing broken limbs. Little patients with more serious fractures that would require lengthy operations were made as comfortable as possible on all the available couches, and given painkillers and sedatives whilst they waited to be taken upstairs to the operating theatres on the top floor.

At one point, as she glanced outside the window she could see the air ambulance helicopter zooming down, preparing to land on the roof with another batch of patients. The helipad was an absolute necessity in these emergency situations when transporting casualties through the London rush-hour traffic would have been a nightmare—not only to the paramedics, but also to the commuters on the roads.

About eight o'clock Edward paged her bleeper and asked if she was free to help him.

'Where are you?' she asked quickly.

'Surgical Outpatients. I've been dealing with the backlog of patients who were in the waiting room when the casualties from the coach crash had to take precedence. Sister Longman, who's been helping me, can't stay any longer. She's got to go home to her family so if Clive could spare you from Orthopaedics...'

'Orthopaedics is quiet again, apart from the little patients waiting to go up to theatre and I've got a couple of good staff nurses in charge of them. I'll just check with Clive but it should be OK.'

Clive didn't seem overjoyed when she announced that Edward needed her help, but he said he would cope.

'We've dealt with all the emergency patients, Clive,' she pointed out. 'So apart from—'

His green eyes flickered. 'Look, I've agreed you should go. The boss has asked for help so you'd better get a move on.'

As she hurried along to the surgical department, she was quietly fuming at the childish way that Clive was behaving. It was almost as if he was jealous of Edward for having a more prestigious job than he had—or maybe he was jealous of something else. Perhaps he imagined that because she and Edward seemed to have a good working relationship this was spilling out into their social life as well.

Which was quite ridiculous, wasn't it? The fact that they were going out for dinner this evening... She felt a pang of despair as she realised they would never make it. Immediately, she checked her feelings, as she thought how insignificant was her disappointment when compared to the trauma that her young patients and their families were going through.

Arriving at Surgical Outpatients, she hurried into the treatment room. Edward was bending over the examination couch, his skilful fingers palpating the abdomen of a small patient whilst the young boy's mother, her face wrinkled with anxiety, watched.

She took up her place at the other side of the examination couch and concentrated all her attention on the tiny figure.

Edward glanced up briefly, before continuing with his examination. 'This is William, Sister. He's five and his tummy's been aching since he woke up this morning. Is that right, William?'

The little boy nodded. His mother leaned forward in her chair. 'I thought he was just playing me up so I sent him to school and then I got this call at work asking me to come and take him to the doctor's. My doctor sent us to Casualty and we were just going to be seen when all the children who'd been on that crashed coach started arriving. To be honest, I think he ate too many sweets last night.'

'Do you like sweets, William?' Amanda asked casually. It was always a good ploy to find out if the child would brighten up at the mention of sweets.

The little boy pulled a face. 'I don't want any sweeties. I want to go home to bed.'

'I'm going to find you a nice bed here in the hospital tonight,' Edward said gently. 'And Mummy can stay too, if she likes.'

Mrs Fairburn looked concerned. 'Is it something serious, Doctor?'

'I'd like to keep William in for observation, Mrs Fairburn. We need to do further tests to find out what's causing the pain. We'll give you a diagnosis as soon as we can, but meanwhile I want you to help us keep William as comfortable as possible in the surgical ward.'

'What do you think is wrong with William?' Amanda asked Edward as they snatched a few minutes away from their work, when their little patient had been settled in a bed on the surgical ward.

Edward took a sip of the coffee that one of the staff nurses had just produced. He leaned back in the chair normally occupied by the surgical consultant as he began to explain his theory about the diagnosis.

'Initially, I thought William had appendicitis. The area

over the whole of the abdomen was tender and his back was painful. But his temperature was only slightly raised and on further investigation I came to the conclusion that we've got a case of ureteric colic.'

'So you think William may have a stone in his waterworks and that's what's causing the pain? Unusual in a child of his age.'

'Exactly! That's why I've ordered a number of tests to check the diagnosis. I've alerted the surgical consultant who's in theatre at the moment and he'll take a look at William as soon as he's free.'

'The stone might be passed down in the urine, mightn't it?'

'That's what I'm hoping. Otherwise, we'll try laser treatment. If there are complications we'll need to operate.'

She put down her coffee-cup on the desk and smiled. 'Do you mean we as in…?'

Edward smiled. 'I like to keep my hand in. Even though I spend most of my time here in Outpatients, I work a few hours a week in the operating theatres. Once a surgeon, always a surgeon.'

She leaned back in her chair, relaxing for the first time that day and feeling the tension drain away as she looked across at Edward.

'Yes, I remember Mrs Drew, our principal nursing officer, mentioning something about it when you first arrived.' She cleared her throat as she prepared to ask the question which had constantly been at the back of her mind. 'Why did you take an administrative post?'

'Why did you?' he countered.

'Difficult to say. I had to work in Outpatients so I can be a real mother to Tom and the extra salary of the higher post is useful, of course, but there's something about climbing the professional ladder that's compulsive, wouldn't you say?'

Edward smiled and leaned forward towards her. 'Perhaps you were searching for power when you left your comfortable niche in the Grayson practice.'

She gave him a wry smile. 'I don't think so. I honestly don't know what I was searching for. I only knew I needed to get away and find myself.'

'And have you succeeded?'

She thought for a moment before shaking her head. 'I think I keep changing. Just when I think I've found out what life is all about something happens to upset the status quo and...'

She paused, not wanting to get in too deep with her philosophical ideas. It was true she was changing all the time, and never more so than since Edward had come back into her life!

He seemed to sense her reluctance to reveal her innermost thoughts as he leaned forward and touched her on the arm. 'You must be tired, Amanda. It's been a long day.'

It certainly had. She stood up and walked towards the window and stood looking out with her back towards Edward. The June sunshine had been high enough in the sky to peep over the top of the tall hospital buildings during the day, but the orange-tinted light was darkening fast. Somewhere out there in the countryside beyond this busy city people would be experiencing a glorious sunset. The sort of sunset she'd watched as a child holding onto her mother's hand in the Yorkshire Dales. Her mother's hand—never her father's!

She would have to make a dutiful trek north to see the parents again soon. Even though the rift caused by her untimely departure from the family fold and her subsequent lifestyle hadn't been healed, they still expected her to visit them occasionally. Whenever she had to face the ordeal, she preferred to go in the summer when the hills and moors would be looking their best.

She felt a momentary pang of nostalgia for the old life, everything taking its predictable course. But she banished the feeling almost as soon as it arose. She'd chosen to strike out on her own and she wasn't doing too badly. And she still had Tom, the jewel in her crown!

She became aware that Edward was now standing behind her, looking out over her head at the darkening scene. An ambulance scurried into the forecourt. A young man, looking decidedly agitated, got out of a car and hurried to wait as the back doors were opened and a stretcher was brought out. The tiny precious form beneath the blanket wasn't moving. Amanda found herself hoping that the team in Accident and Emergency would perform a miracle. Hospital life meant human drama every second of the day.

She swung round, and was surprised to find that Edward was uncomfortably close to her.

Seconds later, she had to admit that uncomfortable wasn't the right word to describe his nearness to her. She was certainly disturbed by it and yet she didn't want him to move away. Looking up, she saw his dark eyes held an expression of something akin to real tenderness. His voice was husky when he spoke.

'I had to cancel the table at the restaurant. I asked them to hold it but they couldn't. It's one of these places where they have a waiting list for cancellations.'

She nodded. 'I'd already realised we would be too late when we finished here.'

And the weariness stealing over her made her think that she wouldn't have had the strength to put on her glad rags, anyway!

He put both hands on her shoulders. 'But we've still

got to have some supper, so maybe you'd like to come back to my place.'

She experienced a cocktail of emotions. His hands on her shoulders were certainly putting her off rational thought but somewhere at the back of her mind she was registering the fact that she was dying to find out where Edward lived. And Alice wasn't expecting her back. Tom would have gone to sleep in Mark's bedroom so she was actually free for as long as...

He dropped his hands to his sides. 'I can see you don't like the idea. OK, then...'

'Oh, but I do!' She knew she'd convinced him by her anxious-to-please voice and wished she'd been a bit more cool about the arrangement. 'I was simply making a mental review of my domestic arrangements.'

'Which are?'

'Well, Tom will be spending the night at Alice's and—'

He smiled. 'So what are we waiting for? Let's go and have some supper.'

He put an arm casually round her shoulders as they went towards the door. She felt a surge of excitement that she didn't know how to cope with. Was it the thought of spending a few hours with a highly attractive man, or the thought of being with Edward himself? Either way, her weariness had completely disappeared and she was raring to go.

In fact, she would have to be careful she didn't go overboard! It was one thing to enjoy an evening with Edward and quite another to allow her emotions to become involved. She'd managed for so long without commitment that she thought perhaps she couldn't cope with it if it reared its ugly head. Her disastrous relationship with Mike had taught her to keep herself uninvolved with the opposite sex.

'Can you cook?' she asked as Edward opened the door for her.

He laughed. 'I can read the instructions on the packets from Marks & Spencer and press the right buttons on the microwave. I keep a supply of instant food in my freezer all ready for my lonely evenings.'

She tried to dampen her feelings of delight at the thought that Edward spent his evenings alone. At least he wasn't going to take her to a family home whilst his wife and children were on holiday. Just exactly where was he taking her?

'It's quite convenient, really,' Edward was explaining as he drove down into the underground car park at the Barbican complex in East London. 'Depends on the traffic, but I usually make it across town in a few minutes.'

'I'm sure you do!'

She ran a hand through her tousled hair. Edward had kept the top down on his zippy car as they had driven across from the hospital. The traffic had been light and he'd been able to keep up a fair speed. The warm June evening had brought out the pedestrian crowds all enjoying the feeling of high summer and Amanda had caught something of the gaiety that prevailed throughout the too often sun-starved London community.

Looking sideways at Edward's profile as he turned the wheel to park the car, she felt her excitement mounting. The journey over here had been fun and she was looking forward to the hour ahead of her. That was all it would be: time to enjoy a light supper and then she would get the tube back—or she might splash out on a cab as it was so late and not too far away to stretch her purse.

Edward's apartment looked out over the enclosed, private gardens of the Barbican complex. Standing at the window, she could see a young couple sitting on a wooden seat. They were very close to each other, getting closer by the second, very young—so very young! A lot younger than she was and they looked so much in love. She wondered what it would be like to fall in love with someone who would love you back, not just for your body but for the whole package that comprised the real you.

She gave a deep sigh of longing, primeval longing, and at that moment Edward called to her from the kitchen.

'If Madame would care to come and examine the menu...?'

She hurried across the close-carpeted room to join him. He was standing by the upright freezer. A blast of cold air hit her as he opened the door.

'What an impressive menu! It looks more like a library!'

Edward laughed. 'Well, choose a title, quickly, and let's get reading, 'cos I'm starving.'

She ran her finger over the side of the boxes that were stacked along the shelves of the upright freezer.

'Mmm, chicken kiev—I love chicken kiev!'

'Chicken kiev coming right up.' He was already unwrapping the packaging and placing it in the microwave before uncorking a bottle of wine and handing her a glass.

'To a good working relationship!' he said, holding out his own glass to chink against hers.

She took a sip of her wine. 'I'd forgotten this was supposed to be a working dinner. What exactly was it that you wanted to discuss? I mean...'

He put his glass down on the kitchen table and put his hands on either side of her arms, pulling her towards him.

'I was only looking for an excuse to spend the evening with you to find out what you're really like away from hospital. I'm a firm believer that you shouldn't mix business with pleasure.'

Very gently, he lowered his head and kissed her on the

lips. Pulling himself away, almost immediately, he looked down at her with an enigmatic expression. 'I didn't mean to kiss you but you looked so enticing that—'

'Enticing?' She glanced down at the decidedly crumpled white shirt and black trousers of her work uniform. There'd been no time to change as Edward had whisked her away from the hospital carrying a holdall that contained the navy blue suit she'd worn that morning. 'You've got a good imagination!'

'It's not imagination,' he said quietly, his voice husky.

She could feel the emotional tension rising. How could she have imagined that she could keep their relationship platonic? The sensual chemistry between them was blatantly obvious. She realised, in a blinding flash, that she'd been attracted to Edward when he'd been working with her father all those years ago, but she hadn't understood the powerful stirrings of her youthful body at the time. But she certainly understood them now, when her body was no longer youthful but in the full flush of womanhood.

She would have to do something before she got carried away by unwelcome ideas. Unwelcome because she didn't want to harbour romantic notions about Edward. She wanted to maintain the status quo; Edward was an old friend from the past and a working colleague. They would have occasional social outings together which she would enjoy and then she would go home and forget all about him whilst she cared for her son and did the ironing and all the other…

When he took her in his arms she wasn't the least bit surprised. Startled, perhaps, and, having meant to resist, she now found herself nestling close against him, revelling in the tremors of excitement that were turning her legs to jelly. If he hadn't been holding her so tightly she felt she would have crumpled to the floor.

This time when he kissed her she gave herself entirely to the thrill of his lips, ignoring the nagging voice of reason that was warning her not to become emotionally involved. Whatever changes were taking place at this particular moment were extremely welcome. And anyway, how could she resist?

An annoyingly persistent pinging sound from the microwave pulled them both up sharp.

He pulled himself away, with a rasping groan. 'We could leave all this and…'

Her lips moved with the rational words that had been planted there by the sensible part of her brain. 'I thought you said you were starving.'

He gave her a rakish grin. 'I was…but…'

He hesitated. She longed for him to hold her in his arms again but knew she'd broken the romantic spell.

Decisively, and, she realised, boringly, she walked over to the microwave and pressed the button that opened the transparent door.

'Here, let me do that.' He removed the container and set it down in the middle of the kitchen table. '*Voilà, Madame.*'

'Where do you keep your knives and forks?'

It was going to be OK! He hadn't really wanted to progress any further—had he? Their platonic friendship was still intact. She'd got what she wanted, which was…?

She'd kept within the guidelines she'd drawn up for herself, based on experience. But that was the traumatising experience of being seduced by a rogue. And Edward was different, or would be different if she ever chose to find out—if he was ever brave enough to invite her negative responses again, which was highly unlikely!

'A delicious supper!' She folded her long legs beneath her on the sofa in the living room as she accepted the coffee-cup from Edward.

'Thanks!' He gave her a wry smile as he settled himself on the sofa beside her. 'I pride myself on my haute cuisine, as you have now discovered.'

She took a sip of her coffee wondering whether—or was she hoping?—he would make some kind of amorous move that would show her he hadn't been put off by her initial cold response.

'Since Tom is sleeping at Alice's, is she expecting you back?'

She hesitated. How would she cope if Edward made passionate advances?

Very badly! She had absolutely no experience and Edward was a much-travelled man of the world.

'No, I don't have to report in,' she said carefully.

He leaned back against the cushions. 'You seem to have your domestic arrangements fully under control. How did you meet up with Alice?'

'Alice moved in to her flat a few weeks before I moved into mine. We both had a one-year-old son and no husband. Alice's husband was a security guard who happened to be in the wrong place at the wrong time. He died of stab wounds when he was fending off a drug-crazed burglar.'

'How awful!'

'Alice was struggling to make ends meet, and I was determined to get some medical qualifications so I could earn a living for Tom and me. I paid Alice to child-mind for Tom when I became a student nurse at St Elizabeth's. Over the years, the arrangement has become more flexible but I've always insisted she take a pay increase when I got one. So it's worked extremely well for both of us.'

'Haven't you had any help from your parents?'

She smiled. 'You know my father. What do you think?'

He nodded. 'You mean he's never forgiven you for giving up your place at medical school and leaving the family fold?'

'He's a very stubborn man. But he still expects me to visit occasionally. Since he and Mum retired he's actually started writing to me. I got a letter only last week telling me they haven't seen me for a long time; the implication being that it's my duty to keep in touch.'

'So when are you going?'

She frowned. 'Oh, I keep putting it off. It's such a long trek up there by train and then bus—if the local bus is still running—and Tom hates the journey and—'

'Why don't I run you both up there one weekend?'

She was completely thrown by the idea. 'Oh, I couldn't possibly…'

'Yes, you could! I'd planned to go up to Yorkshire during the summer and stay at the Coach and Horses in the next village to yours. Do you remember the Coach and Horses?'

She laughed. 'Do I remember it? My father gave me a lecture about the place soon after my eighteenth birthday. I paid a visit there with a couple of school friends to celebrate the end of our exams. One of Dad's patients told him they'd seen me in there and he was furious. It didn't do any good to explain I was drinking cola. Apparently, it didn't go with the image of the doctor's daughter to drink in such a den of iniquity as the Coach and Horses.'

Edward smiled sympathetically. 'Well, I had a great time there when I was off duty! So, I'd already planned to make a nostalgic visit and reserve a bedroom for the night.'

She hesitated. This would be a no-strings-attached arrangement. And it would be an awful lot more pleasant than making the journey by public transport. Shouldn't she take a chance—just this once?

'Well, in that case, I'd be delighted to accept your kind offer of a lift.'

'Good! That's settled, then.'

He stood up and went over to the walnut bureau against the wall that contained shelves from floor to ceiling stacked with books, bric-à-brac and various *objets d'art*. Letting down the flap of the bureau, he pulled out a large black desk diary.

'How about the first weekend in July?'

She delved in her bag and began searching through her personal, social diary. The rest of June and the whole of July were completely blank. 'Looks OK to me but...' She hesitated.

He came over from the bureau and stood looking down at her. 'But what?'

'I know it sounds inhospitable, but will you simply drop Tom and me off at the end of the lane near the house? My father can just about cope with one black sheep turning up, but two...!'

Edward knelt down in front of her and took both her hands. His eyes searched hers. 'That bad when I left, was it?'

Amanda gave a wry smile. 'Let's just say that you were not my father's favourite person. And when I announced I was leaving only a few weeks later, he somehow linked the two of us together as reprobates. He even said he thought you'd been a bad influence on me...'

'And do you think I was?' he asked quietly.

She drew in her breath. 'You certainly influenced me with your independent ways. Whether or not the influence was good or bad, only time will tell.'

He released her hands and stood up. 'Well, that's a cryptic remark if ever I heard one. Anyway, you must be tired, Amanda. I'll run you home now.'

Just when she was beginning to warm to the situation

and think that very possibly she might try to become liberated!

'Edward, I didn't mean to imply that—'

He swung round. 'Don't worry, Amanda. You've been brutally honest with me. I get the picture and it explains your behaviour towards me when I first arrived.'

'My behaviour?'

He gave a wry smile. 'You were decidedly frosty, initially, weren't you?'

He was standing very close to her. She looked up into his dark, expressive eyes. 'Maybe I was. But we got over that, didn't we?'

'I think we're warming to each other,' he said huskily.

And then he kissed her. His lips awakened her dormant sensual emotions. She knew this was only a goodnight kiss but it was powerful enough to sway her resolutions about not becoming involved.

CHAPTER FOUR

'But I told you, Mum, and you agreed I could go.' Tom glared defiantly across the kitchen table.

'You asked me if you could go to scout camp in the summer. But, at the time, you didn't tell me when it was. I'm still waiting to hear…'

Amanda broke off as she realised that she was beginning to sound just like her father! Tom was ten years old, nearly eleven. The last thing he needed was a lecture on communication. And, to be fair to the poor boy, she wasn't the sort of mother who ever had the time to find out what was happening in his life. Most mothers would have followed up their son's casual remark, way back months ago, with a constant stream of enquiries.

She could plead pressure of work in her own case, but she mustn't start accusing Tom of withholding information.

'I'm sorry, Tom,' she said quietly.

Fluffy, purring around her legs under the table, jumped up onto her lap as if sensing that she needed some moral support. Absently, she stroked the long black fur as she struggled to remain calm and objective. She mustn't alienate her son by behaving in the way that she'd been treated by her father whose rule had been law when she was a child.

Tom put down the spoon he'd been waving around above his cereal bowl and watched her warily across the table.

'Well, I'm sorry as well, Mum. I didn't realise it was so important for me to go up and see Grandpa and

Grandma with you. I don't think they'll miss me, really. Grandpa's always picking on me for getting mud on my shoes and all that... Hey, what's so funny?'

Amanda couldn't help smiling. 'Grandpa used to pick on me for that. He can be a bit strict but—'

'Strict? He terrifies me! I'm always glad when—'

'Ah, the moment of truth!'

Fluffy jumped off Amanda's lap and returned to the saucer of milk by the fridge as she raised her voice in excitement again.

'So, three weeks ago, when I told you that Edward had offered to drive us up to Yorkshire, you decided to conveniently forget that you were otherwise engaged.'

Tom grinned. 'I didn't think you'd mind. I thought you and Edward might get on better without me.'

'Get on better? What's that supposed to mean?'

Tom rolled his eyes. 'Look, Mum, I'm not stupid. I could see he fancied you when he brought you back here that day when we were roller blading out front. He put his arm round you, didn't he, and—?'

'Tom, I was in a state of shock at finding—'

'Don't worry, Mum. I think he's great and it's time you had a boyfriend at your age.'

She laughed. 'You mean before I get old and past it.'

'Yeah!' He stood up and came round the table to put his hands loosely around her neck. 'Got to go! Alice said to go upstairs as soon as I was ready and she'll take me swimming with Mark before school.'

'But you didn't—'

'I really did forget to tell you last night. Bye!' He planted a kiss on the side of her cheek. She turned to put her arms round him but he was already nearly at the door.

As she heard him running up the steps to Alice's flat she couldn't help thinking that it seemed only yesterday that she'd held his hand as he'd clung on to the bannister rail with the other. He hadn't wanted her to leave him on that first morning when she'd gone to St Elizabeth's to start her nursing training.

But Alice had soon won him round and over the years had become a second mother to him. And very soon he wouldn't need either of them. Tomorrow, he would be sleeping in a cold field, probably surrounded by cows and maybe the odd hostile bull.

She shivered at the awful thought. As she stood up and carried the cereal bowls over to the sink she made an inward note to get home as early as she could tonight so that she could make sure Tom packed everything he needed for this expedition. And then she would have to do her own packing for the weekend. Usually, she didn't give it a thought until a few minutes before she had to leave. A couple of pairs of knickers, a sweater and a toothbrush were the usual essentials.

But tomorrow would be different. She wanted to wear something casual but trendy for the journey in Edward's zippy car. Supposing they stopped off for a coffee at some posh hotel, or they might even have lunch somewhere. Her parents weren't expecting her until the evening and Edward had suggested they make an early start.

She didn't have a chance to speak to Edward in hospital about their proposed weekend until the end of the afternoon. The morning had been taken up with lengthy meetings and administration, which meant that her usual Friday round of the outpatient departments had to be fitted in after lunch.

Clive Goddard was attending a conference of orthopaedic surgeons so Edward had been running his outpatient department for a couple of days. He looked up and smiled as she went in to see him. Turning to the little patient who was sitting by his desk, he said, 'Look who's come to see us, Timmy.'

'Hi, Sister Grayson!' the little boy said happily. 'Have you come to take my plaster off?'

Amanda looked across at Edward and smiled. 'I'd be delighted to remove your plaster, Timmy, if Mr Burrows…'

'We've been waiting for you to arrive, Sister,' Edward said. 'I knew you were on your way and Timmy had asked if you could be the one who took the plaster off. Isn't that right, Timmy?'

Timmy was getting off the chair. He nodded as he solemnly held his plastered arm towards Amanda. 'I'm ready, Sister.'

Edward followed them into the plaster room.

Her little patient watched, wide-eyed, as she picked up the plaster saw.

Edward leaned forward and held onto the plaster as Amanda peeled it back. As she finished the final cut, he removed it completely and held it up for Timmy to see.

'Can I have it, please?' Timmy reached forward with the hand that had just been released from the plaster.

'Nothing much wrong with your arm now, Timmy,' Edward said, taking hold of the little boy's hand as he examined the forearm.

Amanda ran her fingers the length of Timmy's arm, taking special care to scrutinise the area of the break. 'As good as new!'

Edward did further tests on Timmy's arm and pronounced it perfect.

Amanda put the old plaster cast in a large brown paper bag and handed it to Timmy. 'Do you want to go and show your arm to Mummy and your little brother now?'

Timmy grinned. 'Mummy's going to buy me an ice cream if I'm good. Have I been good, Sister?'

'Angelic!' Edward said.

'Yes, but have I been good?'

Amanda smiled across at Edward as she took hold of the little boy's hand. 'Of course you have.'

She took him back to his mother who was in the waiting room, sitting beside the play area. Craig, Timmy's little two-year-old brother, was the reason that his mother was unable to accompany him when he went in to see the doctor. Once Craig had been shown into the play area with its building bricks, plastic cars, bouncy castle and numerous other toys of all shapes and sizes he didn't want to leave. And it was easier for the medical staff to treat Timmy on his own rather than with a restless little brother beside him.

Amanda had made a rule about the play area which was that mothers should stay with their children until it was time for them to go in to see the doctor. Sometimes a mother would ask one of the outpatient nurses if she could go off and have a cup of tea. If their child or children were playing happily then there was no problem, but the nurse who'd given permission had to keep her eye on the children left behind.

Amanda was pleased with the way the play area was working. It had been one of her innovations. She'd noticed how difficult it was for mothers with more than one child to attend Outpatient clinics so she'd put the proposal forward to the board of governors and been granted a sizeable sum to set it up. It had been known, during the few weeks that it had been up and running, for mothers to come in a couple of hours before their child's appointment simply to enjoy the play area.

'I've made an appointment for Timmy with the physiotherapy department,' Amanda told his mother. 'And we'd like to see you again in a couple of months.'

Timmy clung to Amanda's hand. 'Will you be working in this bit?'

Amanda smiled. 'I'll come and see you,' she promised, and made a note to put it in her desk diary when she got back to her room.

As she hurried back to see Edward it occurred to her that her professional diary was always better organised than her personal diary. She'd got used to having few and far between social engagements that were easy to remember in her head, but now that Tom was growing up she would have to keep track of all the events he was supposed to attend.

Edward was typing Timmy's notes into the computer when she got back to the consulting room. It was important that Clive should have a full record of what had happened in his absence. Edward swung round in his chair.

'Did Timmy get his ice cream?'

'I told his mother he'd been excellent, so he'll probably get two. I left him bouncing up and down on the bouncy castle with his little brother.'

'I must say the play area was a great idea of yours.'

She smiled. Praise from the boss was always welcome. 'Thanks. There always was a small play corner with a few books and a couple of boxes of small plastic toys, but I felt we needed something that would really keep the children occupied.'

She hesitated. 'Edward...'

'Yes?'

She suddenly felt unusually shy. It had been OK to accept a lift up to Yorkshire when she had thought Tom was going to be with them, but now that it was just the two of them...

'Tom can't come with us,' she said quickly. 'He's going to scout camp for the weekend.'

Edward swung his chair back again and seemed to be

concentrating on the computer screen as he tapped in another sentence. When he'd finished, he stood up, looking down at her with a quizzical expression.

'That won't be a problem for you, will it? I mean, had you hoped to use him as a chaperon?'

'Certainly not! I...'

He gave her a wry grin. '"The lady doth protest too much, methinks"...'

'There's no need to quote Shakespeare at me,' she said evenly, but she could see the funny side of the situation. 'Well, all it means is that you really will have to keep out of sight of my parents otherwise they'll jump to embarrassing conclusions.'

His dark, expressive eyes flickered. 'Such as?'

'Well, they might think we—'

'With me in a hotel room and you locked up in your ivory tower! I couldn't even get a room in the next village. When I phoned the Coach and Horses, they said they didn't do bed and breakfast any more, so I've made a reservation at a hotel in Leeds.' He smiled. 'If we'd wanted a quiet weekend together we wouldn't have chosen to trek up to see your parents, would we?'

She struggled to control the blush that was spreading, infuriatingly, across her cheeks. 'Of course not.'

Since that evening in Edward's apartment at the Barbican when she'd made it quite clear that she wanted a platonic friendship, his attitude towards her had been cool to friendly. Their working relationship had been efficient and their social relationship non-existent. During the last three weeks she'd had time to assess the situation and she'd wished that she could have somehow conveyed to him that she wasn't completely discounting the possibility of them becoming closer.

It was just that, having been badly hurt the first time, she found it so hard to trust again. Looking up at Edward now, she thought that this would be a man she could trust. But would he give her another chance?

She cleared her throat. 'So what time shall we leave in the morning?'

'I'll pick you up about nine,' he said briskly.

The scouts' Land Rover was turning out of the forecourt as Edward tried to negotiate the entrance to the flats. Watching from the front door, Amanda saw Tom lean out through the open window and wave to Edward.

She felt a moment of panic. Edward was early and she wasn't ready! She'd have to invite him in to witness the early-morning chaos.

Edward waved back, keeping one hand on the wheel as he drove towards the front door. He stepped out and Amanda, running a hand over her short auburn hair, still wet from the shower, went to meet him.

'It's just as well we haven't got Tom with us,' he said as he stepped out of the car. 'There's not much passenger and luggage space in this car. He would have had to sit in the tiny seat behind us.'

'It's a beautiful-looking model but it's not intended to be a family car,' Amanda said, turning to go back inside.

He was right behind her as she ran up the stairs. 'It's perfect for me, because I'm not a family man.'

She turned to face him on the landing, the key to her flat poised in her fingers.

'So you were never tempted to leave your idyllic state of bachelorhood?' she said lightly. It was the question she'd wanted to ask ever since Edward had come back into her life. 'I mean, you're thirty-seven, a much-travelled man. There must have been times when...'

He leaned forward and, taking the key from her hand, he turned it in the lock.

'Put it this way,' he said carefully. 'I've got nothing to

come back for. I've lived a full life and, yes—in answer to your question, I did commit myself but—'

'Hi, Amanda!'

What bad timing! Amanda turned and, looking up the stairs, saw Alice coming down, followed by Mark. Another second and she might have learned something more about Edward's mysterious past. Still, she had all weekend to coax something out of him.

She put on a bright smile for her friend. 'Hello, Alice. I've just been downstairs to see Tom off to scout camp.'

She hovered in her open doorway as she watched Edward stepping forward and extending his hand towards Alice.

'I'm Edward. So you're the lady who makes Amanda's life easier.'

Dark-haired Alice was smiling up at Edward, a blatant expression of admiration on her high cheek-boned face. Amanda basked in the reflected glory because Edward was looking particularly handsome today in his casual jeans worn with an open-necked cotton shirt.

'We both make life easier for each other,' Alice said, still holding onto Edward's hand as if mesmerised by his dark eyes. 'I don't know what I'd do without Amanda to help me out.'

'I'm going to join the scouts after the summer holidays, aren't I, Mum?' Mark said.

Alice smiled. 'You certainly are.'

Turning back, she confided in Edward, 'Mark's more cautious than Tom. He lets Tom test things out and then if it's OK he joins in. He's rather like me, I suppose. I'm naturally shy whereas Amanda just oozes confidence. That's why she's a successful career girl and I'm just a mum.'

'But a very good mum,' Amanda said quickly.

She always tried to boost Alice's confidence whenever

she could. Lately, she'd noticed that her friend seemed to be becoming restless. She'd even talked about trying to get a job but seemed to have shelved the idea for the moment. It would certainly complicate matters if they were both working, but she would cross that bridge when she came to it.

Alice and Mark continued on their way down the stairs to the ground floor.

'Well, mustn't keep you two from your weekend away,' Alice called. 'Don't worry about Fluffy. I've got plenty of milk and cat food. Have a good time!'

'We will!' Edward said as he followed Amanda into her flat.

Since she'd got up she'd been busy assembling Tom's kit: plastic plate, knife, fork and spoon, mug, sleeping bag, sweater, clean socks, underpants and all the other essentials on the list he'd finally presented to her. She'd had to go out to the supermarket yesterday evening for the late-night shopping to get everything he wanted. But her own bag was still empty apart from her toothbrush and a couple of pairs of knickers.

'I'll be about ten minutes,' she said. 'Would you like me to make you a coffee while you wait?'

'I'll do it. Would you like a cup?'

'Yes, please.' She scuttled away into her bedroom, hoping he would ignore the mess in the sink. For a confirmed bachelor it would be a bit off-putting to be confronted by her breakfast chaos.

She decided to wear her linen trouser suit. It was smart enough for her parents to approve of but still casual enough for a weekend in the country. The weather report had promised a warm, dry weekend so she added a cotton dress—the one her mother had actually approved of during her last visit—to her holdall, but left out her raincoat.

Edward looked up when she emerged from the bedroom, carrying her bag. 'Good! You're not taking too much luggage. I had visions of having to fix a roof-rack, in which case we couldn't keep the top down. You have got a scarf for your hair, I hope?'

'Of course. Will it be terribly windy when we get on the motorway?'

He laughed. 'You'll soon find out.'

'Not too windy for you, is it?' he called over the noise of the traffic and the rushing air currents.

Amanda was retying the knot on her scarf which had kept slipping during the first part of their journey.

'It's great!' she shouted back. 'Most exhilarating!'

She loved the feel of the wind rushing around the car and the sun shining down on them. The only drawback as far as she was concerned was that it was difficult to keep up a conversation. And there were so many questions she was dying to ask Edward. This would have been the perfect time to find out more about him!

Would she get a chance over lunch—presuming they were going to have some lunch? Perhaps Edward was planning to deposit her at her parents' and go off for the entire weekend on his own—or meet up with an old friend. That was an even more disturbing thought. She'd better find out before her curiosity got the better of her.

'Are we going straight to…?'

'As I wasn't able to book a room at the Coach and Horses, I thought we'd have lunch there.'

Amanda laughed with relief. It was almost as if Edward had been reading her thoughts because they had both started to speak at the same moment.

Edward was negotiating a roundabout as he turned off the motorway. 'What's so funny?'

'I was just about to ask you what you were planning to do with me.'

'I'd been reading your mind.'

'I hope not!'

'Wicked thoughts?'

'No more than usual.'

'Ouch!' He pulled up just in time as a sheep ambled across the road. 'These country roads can be so dangerous!'

'Idyllic countryside round here, but you mustn't relax on the roads.'

She looked up at the fells in the distance. The sun shining on the high peaks gave them a golden glow. All around her, in the lower reaches of the hills, the sheep were cropping the grass. Above them, on the moors, the birds swooped down over the heather, calling to each other in a celebration of high summer.

She felt a sudden rush of nostalgia now that she was back in home territory. She'd chosen to leave this beautiful part of England but it was still in her blood.

'I love coming home,' she said quietly. 'But I'm happy to go away again at the end of the visit.'

She felt his hand close over hers and a tingle of excitement ran through her. It was so wonderful that the two of them had known each other in those far-off days when they'd both been trying to find out what life was all about. She realised that Edward had influenced her so much and now here he was, still part of her life. This warm feeling she had about him was pure nostalgia—wasn't it? Or was it something else?

Glancing sideways, analysing that strong, confident, handsome profile, she couldn't hold back the idea that she might be getting in too deep. She remembered how she'd always admired Edward, right from that very first day when her father had introduced him. She knew exactly where she'd been standing—by the window-seat in the sitting room—when her father had brought his new trainee in and she'd thought, Wow!

Something had stirred inside her and she hadn't known what it was—but she knew now! Without a shadow of a doubt she'd had a teenage crush on Edward even though she'd tried to ignore it. But how could she analyse the way she was feeling now? It was more than a teenage crush, wasn't it? Was this what it felt like to fall in love?

He removed his hand, needing both hands on the wheel to negotiate a difficult uphill bend that led to the valley where Amanda had been born. She looked anxiously down the road leading to her village as they drove past it, hoping she wouldn't see her father or mother driving up to claim her attention before she'd had lunch with Edward.

He pulled up in front of the building which had been the Coach and Horses and they looked at each other in surprise.

'It's changed,' Amanda said. 'It's bigger. And what does that sign say?'

Edward turned off the engine and leaned forward to get a better look at the discreet, brass plate beside the door.

'The Coach House Restaurant. Let's go and investigate.'

The exterior of the pub was painted gold and cream, whereas she remembered it had always been a dour shade of brown or black. A conservatory extension on the side looked as if it might be a large dining room.

Edward climbed over the top of his door and came round to Amanda's side to help her out.

'It looks as if it's been gentrified,' he said solemnly.

Amanda laughed. 'Shall we find out?'

The information in the glass case at the side of the door informed them that the establishment had been awarded three stars in a prestigious guide to restaurants and table reservations were advised. Clients were also requested not to park their cars in the front of the building. There was a large car park at the rear of the premises, apparently.

Edward groaned as he decided he'd better comply. 'This shouldn't take a minute.'

Amanda strolled inside whilst he was reparking the car and found her way to the pink and gold ladies' room. She'd been dying to go to the loo for the last twenty miles but had been, uncharacteristically, too embarrassed to request a comfort stop. So she'd crossed her legs and taken deep breaths of the bracing country air.

This place certainly had been gentrified! There were small fluffy hand towels and sweet-smelling soap—so different from the facilities in the tiny, very basic, outside loo across the cobbled yard which she remembered from her teenage years.

Emerging with newly applied lipstick and combed hair, she found Edward waiting for her in front of the reception desk. The girl in charge of reservations was frowning as Edward asked about lunch.

The snooty receptionist didn't quite tap their hands for failing to make a reservation, but she conveyed the impression that she would like to. After a lengthy consultation over her internal phone, she grudgingly admitted that she might be able to twist the head waiter's arm and find them a table.

'It's certainly changed since you could sit on a stool by the bar and order a ploughman's lunch,' Amanda whispered to Edward as a waiter showed them to a starched-white-clothed table, with silver cutlery gleaming in the sunlight, by the window.

Edward put his hand across the table and took hold of hers. 'It's fun having you with me, Amanda.'

'Are you ready to order, sir?'

Edward's hand remained firmly around hers. 'Not yet,'

he told the waiter. 'We'll have a bottle of champagne while we're making up our minds.'

'Will you be able to drive afterwards, Edward?' Amanda asked as the waiter scurried away.

'I thought we'd have a walk after lunch. I'm not planning to take you home until this evening. Does that fit in with your plans?'

'Perfectly!' She watched the waiter removing the foil from the neck of the bottle, fiddling with the cork, easing it out until the controlled explosive sound sent her even further into party mood.

'Here's to our weekend,' Edward said, raising his glass towards her.

She took a sip and the bubbles tickled her nose. She giggled. 'Pity they haven't got bedrooms here. It's quite nice when you get past the reception area.'

He gave her a rakish grin. 'What are you suggesting?'

'Oh, nothing!' she said quickly. 'I meant it would have been nice to know that you were only over in the next village. You're going to have to travel miles over to your hotel in Leeds.'

'I don't mind. I've got nothing else to do with my weekend.'

'Don't you ever get lonely?' she asked, emboldened by the first rush of Dutch courage from her champagne.

'Never! I love being on my own. When you've extricated yourself from a disastrous marriage you know when you're well off… Are you going to decide what you'd like to eat?'

She found it difficult to concentrate on the menu, having at last elicited some information from Edward about his past life. Eventually, she made up her mind and chose to start with eggs florentine, described as poached egg on a bed of spinach with a cheese sauce, followed by woodpigeon with wild mushrooms.

The spinach starter was delicious and required all her attention, so she was halfway through her succulent main course before she plucked up courage to ask any more questions.

'So how long were you married?'

Edward gave a bitter laugh. 'Too long! Long enough to realise I'd never get myself tied up again.'

She toyed with a piece of mushroom. 'Was it that bad?'

He put down his fork and faced her across the table. 'Not in the beginning. Not while Melissa was still in love with the novelty of being married. We were living in Singapore and I was working long hours to keep her in the manner to which she'd become accustomed. Her father was a very successful international businessman. Melissa had been born out there and had developed expensive tastes.'

He paused, as if unwilling to go on with the unpleasant memories.

'But didn't you know what she was like when you decided to get married?'

He thought for a few seconds. 'To be honest, I don't think I did. I was in love and I didn't look any further than the fact that we enjoyed ourselves together. And Melissa was a very beautiful girl—still is, I expect.'

Amanda ran a hand over her hair, experiencing a sudden feeling of insecurity. No one had ever described her as a very beautiful girl. How could she ever compete with…but did she want to compete with…?

'We had a whirlwind romance. It hadn't occurred to me that she wouldn't take kindly to living on a junior doctor's salary.'

'Didn't she have a job?'

'You must be joking! Girls like Melissa don't work. When would they find the time? They don't get up until midday when it's time to go out for a lettuce-leaf lunch.

Then they have to go shopping, visit the health and beauty salon and prepare for a party in the evening.'

He pushed a piece of steak round his plate, before cutting into it with strong, surgeon-like strokes of his knife.

She watched his furrowed brow and determined movements. He was obviously locked in memories. 'You look as if you're feeling vicious about something.'

He gave her a wry smile. 'I'm taking out my frustration on this piece of meat.'

'Frustration?'

'Perhaps that's not quite the right word,' he said carefully. 'Melissa was always keen on the sexual side of our marriage.'

Amanda felt a pang of envy. She wished she hadn't asked. She didn't want to know any more details but she'd opened the floodgates and she couldn't stop the flow of his reminiscences.

'I think powerless is what I felt when I discovered that Melissa simply hadn't a clue how to consider anyone but herself. We'd married for better or worse and it was getting worse by the minute. I discovered she'd been unfaithful with one of my colleagues at the hospital where I was working only six weeks after the wedding. I tried to forgive her, but when it happened again with someone else I realised that this was going to be the pattern of our lives.'

The waiter had arrived to clear away the plates and Amanda thought she would try to change the subject.

'Did you enjoy your work at the hospital in Singapore?' she said in a bright, conversational tone.

'Very much. But it wasn't leading anywhere. I would have still been in the same position if Melissa hadn't goaded me.'

The waiter had pushed a loaded dessert trolley to the

side of their table. Amanda chose strawberries and cream; Edward asked for a *crème caramel*.

She waited until the waiter had departed before asking, 'How did Melissa goad you?'

He swallowed a piece of *crème caramel* before replying in a deadpan, even tone. 'She was always suggesting I should get a better-paid job. She wanted me to go into business. She said her father would help me to get the right contacts if I asked.'

'And did you—ask, I mean?'

'Of course not! I knew when to opt out of general practice but I'd never doubted the profession I chose. I told Melissa I wasn't going to stay as a junior doctor all my life. I planned to go back to London and study for my fellowship so that I could become a consultant. I'd been thinking about it for some time, but my marriage had held me back. When Melissa taunted me, saying I had no ambition, I knew I had to go for it.'

'And she didn't want to come to London with you?'

He put down his spoon and gave a harsh laugh. 'And spend years waiting around while I worked and studied? Anyway, by this time we'd agreed that our marriage had been a mistake. She's married to a multinational company director now and…'

He broke off. 'Look, this is all very depressing. I didn't mean to unburden myself on you. I hope I'm not curdling the cream on your strawberries.'

She could feel the tension draining away from her as she saw Edward smiling again.

'I was the one who asked for the gory details. It seems that neither of us had much luck first time round.'

'You mean only time around, don't you? Could you contemplate all that agony again? I know I couldn't.'

'You forget—I was never actually married.'

He was looking at her with an expression of tenderness

now. She found herself wishing they were completely alone, so that he could hold her in his arms and they could give each other mutual support for their collective emotional wounds.

'I expect marriage could be a good experience if you're with the right person,' he said quietly. 'But if you're chained to the wrong person it's agony. Like a prison sentence, really.'

'But you broke out of your prison and made a successful life on your own.'

'On my own,' he repeated, almost to himself. 'Surrounded by people all day and returning to my bachelor pad in the evenings.'

He looked up and gave her a deliberately bright smile as if to ease the tension. 'Let's go for that walk.'

CHAPTER FIVE

As Amanda reached the top of the steep path, she leaned against a large warm rock to catch her breath. Edward, several paces in front, turned round and smiled.

'It's a tough old climb, but it's worth it for the view, don't you think?'

She took a deep breath. 'And the air's like wine. Mmm... It's like being on top of the world.'

Looking down into the valley, she could see the Coach House Restaurant, nestling like a doll's house amid tiny trees that looked as if they'd been planted by a child in a miniature garden. She pointed down.

'The cars in the restaurant car park look like Tom's toy cars.'

Edward laughed. 'And there's a toy farm down there with what looks like plastic sheep—except they're moving about, cropping the green carpet. It's good to get away from London, isn't it?'

He was standing right next to her now, resting his hand on the rock she was leaning against. For a few moments neither of them spoke as they listened to the occasional sound of a sheep bleating on the hillside and the excited cries of the crows as they swooped down over the edge of the hill, hovering in the warm currents of air that rose up from the valley.

'Standing here, I feel as if I haven't got a care in the world,' Amanda said, half to herself.

Edward's arms closed around her and he looked down with a sensitive expression in his dark eyes. 'Remember this feeling when you're rushed off your feet next week.'

She looked up into his eyes and saw real tenderness and she knew, at that moment, that she'd fallen in love— in real love. Not the sort of lustful emotion that Mike had created when he'd introduced her to her first relationship. But as soon as the revelation came to her in a blinding flash, she knew she'd better stifle it. Edward was enjoying his bachelor status. She didn't want to frighten him away.

He tightened his arms around her as he leaned down to kiss her, oh, so gently on the lips. His kiss sent shivers of desire running down her spine. Yes, she would remember standing here with Edward, surrounded by all this beauty, for the rest of her life. Just as she could still remember the first moment she'd met him at home.

At the thought of home, she was brought back to reality. 'We ought to be starting back, Edward. My parents will—'

'In a little while. We didn't struggle up here to simply turn round and go back again.'

He knelt down and created a cosy hollow amongst the heather. Taking her hand, he pulled her down beside him until she was lying with her head in the crook of his arm.

'Mmm, this is the life,' he said huskily, closing his eyes and leaning his head against Amanda's.

She closed her eyes, revelling in the warmth of the sun on her face. The rapport between them was very precious at that moment. She remained absolutely still and silent, not wanting to shatter the feeling by talking. She felt him stir beside her and opened her eyes. He was looking down at her.

She gave him a shy smile, shy because she didn't know how to handle the confused emotions that were coursing through her. And then he kissed her. This time his kiss deepened into a passionate embrace that swept her along on a tide of delicious sensations. Her body felt as if it would melt as she moulded herself against him, revelling in the liquid sensations that were welling up inside her.

He was pulling himself away from her and she heard his rasping breath as he sat up. 'I think we'd better go back,' he said, his voice husky with emotion. 'Before I get carried away and ravish you here among the heather.'

His voice was light; he was trying to turn the experience into a joke, but she'd recognised that his arousal was as deep as her own. And this time, there had been real emotion—a sharing, caring sort of feeling that she longed to recapture.

He was standing up, holding out his hand towards her. 'Come along, you wicked temptress!'

She laughed. So long as Edward could joke about their feelings for each other they wouldn't have to take them any further. And that was what she wanted, too—wasn't it? She didn't want to spoil their friendship with complicated emotions that required satisfying; emotions that would mean they had to reassess their lives and consider making all sorts of difficult changes.

As she began to follow Edward down the path she told herself that they were both happy with their lives. Neither of them wanted to change direction so she'd better stop dreaming and be realistic.

The restaurant car park was almost empty when they arrived back to claim the car.

'What will you do with yourself in Leeds tonight?' Amanda asked, in a casual tone, as Edward drove out into the main road.

'Maybe go to a concert or see a film.'

Neither of them spoke for a while, each wrapped up in their own thoughts. Amanda was wishing she could stay in the car and go over to Leeds with him. She was beginning to feel apprehensive. It was always a daunting experience facing up to her family and trying to convince them that she was happy and fulfilled with the life she'd chosen.

'You'd better drop me at the end of our road,' she said as they drove down towards her village.

Too late, she saw a familiar car driving towards them. Too bad they were in an open-topped car! She tried to make herself smaller in the seat, but her mother had already seen her and was slowing to a halt, waving one arm in the air.

Edward stopped the car so that the two vehicles were alongside each other.

'Amanda! Where have you been? We expected you an hour ago. I thought you'd be coming by bus from the station. I've been down to the bus stop twice and—'

'Sorry, Mum. I got the chance of a lift so...'

A car ground to a halt behind Edward's car and the driver gave a loud blast on the horn.

'We're blocking the road, Amanda,' her mother said. 'Bring your friend in for a cup of tea, won't you?'

The second honking of the horn behind them meant that Edward had to move quickly. Amanda's mother was doing a complicated three-point turn involving an open gateway into a field. Edward pulled over on to the grass verge at the side of the road and waited for her to catch up with them.

'Mum hasn't recognised you,' Amanda said. 'I could get into her car and you could make your escape. As I told you, my father still bears a grudge about the way you took up three months of his time and then left him with another trainee to break in, as he always puts it.'

Edward laughed. 'Oh, don't be so melodramatic! I don't care what your parents thought about me giving up my GP training. I've had a great life so far and I don't regret my decision.'

'I wish I could be as positive as you,' she said quietly. 'I don't think my parents are convinced by the show I put on for them every time I come up here.'

He put his hand over hers. 'My advice is to just be your own charming self, Amanda.'

She gave him a wry smile. 'Easier said than done. When I go through the doorway I'm turned back into the dutiful daughter.'

'Well, this time, I'll be with you when you cross the threshold so pluck up courage and don't change your attitude. You're a highly successful career woman, the mother of a wonderful, intelligent son that any grandparents would be proud of.'

She felt a warm glow stealing over her. Put like that, she didn't feel as if she'd failed her parents in any way. 'Thanks, Edward. I once vowed that, if I ever met you again, I'd never listen to your advice.'

'Funny how life turns out, isn't it? I never expected to meet you again.'

'Neither did I,' she replied quickly, trying not to acknowledge that she was misleading herself again. She'd always hoped that she might meet up with Edward somewhere in the world. Edward had gone for a job involving travel; following his example, she'd decided to travel and see the world. But the world was a bigger place than she had imagined in those far-off days.

'There's Mum!'

Edward let in the clutch and followed Amanda's mother to the turning that led down to the surgery.

'Your house looks bigger than I remember it,' Edward said as he switched off the engine.

'It's been extended over the years to cope with the expansion of the practice. Fortunately, Dad employed a good architect and a skilful builder so the extensions are in keeping with the rest of the house.'

Edward swung his long legs over the side of the door. Moving swiftly around to the front of the car, he opened the passenger door for Amanda to extricate herself.

She was feeling decidedly self-conscious as she saw her mother coming over from her car. Had she recognised Edward as the young man her father always quoted as an example of the reprobate medical students of today? The fact that the incident was in the past hadn't changed her father's story.

'Good afternoon, Dr Grayson,' Edward said in an unusually polite tone as he held out his hand to Amanda's mother.

'Have we met somewhere before?'

'Edward Burrows. I was a trainee GP here about twelve years ago and—'

'Ah, yes, now I remember you.'

Felicity Grayson's expression didn't change. Only her daughter noted the pink flush spreading around the high neckline of her mother's blouse and recognised that the encounter was causing her some embarrassment. Amanda wondered if she was considering withdrawing the offer of a cup of tea.

Her mother seemed to have come to a decision as she put on a bright, polite smile. 'Well, you'd better come in. My husband will be waiting for his tea.'

She brushed her cheek against Amanda's. 'Lovely to see you again. Did you have a good journey?'

As Amanda assured her mother, in polite tones, that the journey had been most enjoyable, she recognised that she was already adopting the dutiful daughter act, from which she'd so thankfully escaped in a former life.

She gained confidence from the fact that Edward was right behind her as she followed her mother in through the wide stone porch, and along the familiar quarry-tiled passageway that led to the sitting room. She sensed, once again, the special feeling that permeated ancient buildings that had witnessed the happiness and sadness of many generations. The house was over four hundred years old and had been in the family since her grandfather had first set up his surgery there.

As they all went into the sitting room Amanda saw her father standing by the window, his back towards them. He was wearing his old Harris tweed jacket, the one he called his smoking jacket, even though he'd never smoked. It had always signified that he was off duty and woe betide anyone who tried to call him out.

Somehow, he looked as if he'd shrunk. There was a distinct stoop about his shoulders that she hadn't noticed last time she'd been up here. He was definitely beginning to show his age, whereas her mother was still slim and lithe and could easily pass for someone in her fifties, ten years younger.

'Look who's here, Geoffrey!' Felicity Grayson said in a bright, social voice. 'You remember Edward Burrows, don't you?'

'Good afternoon, sir.' Edward, polite as ever, moved forward to shake the bewildered doctor by the hand.

'Hello, Daddy,' Amanda said, kissing the side of his cheek.

For a moment her father seemed as if he'd been struck dumb. When he finally spoke he enunciated his words carefully.

'What's this? A convention of the black sheep?'

'Geoffrey!' Felicity Grayson was beside herself with indignation.

Amanda knew that one of the things her mother couldn't stand was rudeness. Even after all these years together, she was still trying to stop her husband from making his caustic comments.

But Edward appeared completely unmoved. 'That's

very good, sir! I'm glad you've still got your sense of humour. Amanda and I are actually working together at St Elizabeth's Hospital. Amazing that the two of us, with so much in common, should have met up again, don't you think?'

'Incredible!' Dr Grayson conceded dryly. 'Although I have to admit that when Amanda left home so soon after you'd thrown up your job prospects I wondered if you might have persuaded her to run away with you. What exactly do you do at the hospital?'

'Edward is our consultant in charge of Outpatients,' Amanda put in quickly.

'Is he, indeed?'

Amanda could see that her father was clearly impressed.

'So you didn't drop out of medicine, then?' Dr Grayson left the place by the window where he'd been rooted to the spot and advanced further into the middle of the room.

'Of course not! That was never my intention, as I told you at the time. I'd simply come to the conclusion that the restrictions of general practice were not for me.'

It was painfully obvious to Amanda that Edward's patience would run out very shortly.

'I'll get the tea, Mum,' she said. As she headed out towards the kitchen she could hear her father interrogating Edward.

'What do you mean by restrictions? I've never found general practice restricting. In fact...'

She didn't wait around to hear the rest of the sentence. Edward would be able to match up to her father's argumentative nature.

Her mother followed her into the kitchen. 'We'll use the rosebud cups, dear, as it's a special occasion.'

Amanda raised an eyebrow. 'What's special about it?'

'It's always special when you come to visit us. I was

so disappointed when Geoffrey told me that Tom couldn't come. He didn't tell me you'd phoned yesterday until we were having lunch today.'

'And did he forget to tell you I was coming by car?'

Felicity Grayson gave a wry smile. 'He did. In fact he's forgetting more and more nowadays.'

Amanda began setting the cups and saucers out on a tray.

'But he hasn't forgotten Edward,' she said wryly.

'I don't think he'll ever forget Edward!'

Felicity took the kettle from the top of the wood-burning stove and poured boiling water into the teapot to warm it. Amanda eyed her mother as she rearranged the cups, placing silver teaspoons in the saucers. The routine of tea in the afternoon hadn't changed since she was a child.

There was the sound of tyres scrunching on the gravel drive.

'That will be Yvonne,' Felicity said, pouring away the warming water down the sink before spooning tea leaves into the teapot.

Amanda could see her mother counting the number of spoonfuls. One for each person and one for the pot! The tea ritual seemed to require as much concentration as the emergency operations she'd watched her mother perform in the surgery. It took a lot longer than her brief ritual with a tea bag and a mug of hot water. But wasn't that one of the reasons why she'd left home? To have the freedom to do things her own way.

She could hear Yvonne's steps in the hall and a wave of apprehension swept over her. She loved her sister dearly, but she hadn't approved of the way Amanda had flouted convention, as she so often put it. Leaving home she could have forgiven, apparently, but returning, with a child and unmarried!

'Who owns the fantastic car out there?'

Yvonne swept into the kitchen, pushing a strand of fair hair back into the tight, no-nonsense, purposeful knot at the back of her head.

'Hello, Yvonne.' Amanda kissed the air at the side of Yvonne's cheek. 'The car belongs to my escort.'

Yvonne's thin, somewhat severe-looking face broke out into a smile. She sank down into the chair at the side of the ancient fireplace, hitching her cotton skirt up around her knees. Kicking off her heavy duty shoes, she regarded her younger sister with an expression bordering on affection.

'So you've got yourself a boyfriend at last! How does young Tom—?'

'Don't jump to conclusions!' Amanda interrupted hastily. 'One of my colleagues at the hospital was driving up here so he gave me a lift. I think you'll remember him. It's—'

'Edward Burrows, Yvonne!' her mother put in acidly. 'You know, the ex-trainee who infuriated your father when he walked out after—'

'He didn't walk out!' Amanda said, feeling that any minute now she would explode with impatience.

She'd been hanging on to her dutiful daughter persona. Very soon, she would take Edward's advice and become her real self again and then all hell would break loose!

'He gave adequate notice that he didn't want to continue in general practice.'

She slammed shut the fridge door and, desperately trying to control her trembling hands, she poured milk into the bone china milk jug, before glancing at her sister.

'Mum's invited Edward in for a cup of tea, so I hope you'll make him feel welcome, Yvonne. Dad's treating the occasion like the Spanish Inquisition.'

Picking up the tea tray, she marched out of the kitchen.

As she strode along to the sitting room she was hoping she'd left her sister open-mouthed with admiration that she should have made such a bold speech in front of their mother. But, knowing her sister as she did, she expected it would all be water off a duck's back. Yvonne didn't care for any show of histrionics and would simply ignore it.

She pushed open the sitting room door with some trepidation at what she might find. Over the years, this ancient room must have witnessed some angry scenes—threats of pistols at dawn and...

The sight that greeted her made her stop dead in her tracks. To her amazement, she found the two men deep in conversation about the pros and cons of radiation therapy in cancer treatment. Edward looked up from his place on the sofa next to her father and gave her an almost imperceptible wink.

She set the tray down on the central coffee-table and began pouring out, carefully straining the leaves through the silver tea strainer as she'd been taught to do when she was knee-high to a grasshopper.

Yvonne came in looking completely unperturbed and was introduced, unnecessarily, by her father.

'Yvonne is the senior partner of the practice now that we're both retired, Edward,' Geoffrey Grayson said, unable to disguise the pride he felt for his elder daughter. 'We have two junior partners, but no trainee at the moment—thank God! The trouble I've had over the years.'

He gave a loud guffaw of laughter and Edward joined in. It was all too good to be true! Edward and her father sharing a joke at Edward's expense! Amanda served the tea, careful not to spill a drop in any of the saucers. Her father couldn't abide messy saucers and she didn't want anything to spoil the congenial atmosphere.

'So what are your plans for this evening, Edward?' Felicity asked evenly.

'I shall drive over to Leeds to stay in a hotel.'

'Have you got a reservation over there?' Geoffrey put in quickly.

'Yes, I—'

'Cancel it. Stay here. Not much fun for you on your own in a hotel.'

Amanda saw the look that passed between her parents and the silent approval of her mother at the suggestion.

'You could have your old room over the stables,' Felicity said.

'Oh, I couldn't possibly put you to any trouble.'

'It's no trouble. Mrs Brown, my daily help, keeps it aired and ready for visiting students and so forth. You're most welcome. Besides, the chicken casserole I've prepared is far too big for family supper, now that Tom's not coming.'

'And it would be a wicked waste to give Tom's share to the cat,' Geoffrey said wryly.

Amanda was experiencing a mixture of relief that a truce had been reached and apprehension at what could happen if Edward actually did swallow his pride and stay the night. She fully expected that he would drain his teacup and escape to the bright lights.

But how wrong could you get? She watched him smiling at her mother in his most charming manner and accepting her kind invitation.

'Quite like old times!' Yvonne remarked as she perched on the arm of the sofa, beside her father.

Except that Edward and I have changed beyond recognition, Amanda thought. And you can't put the clock back. She would try to relax and not take exception to seemingly innocent remarks during supper. Her father's form of barbed humour would be endured with the impeccable manners that had been drummed into her over the years.

In the event, she needn't have worried about the family supper. The two men engaged in earnest conversation about medical matters throughout the meal whilst her mother and sister wanted to know all about her new job and how Tom was coping with having a high-powered mum.

She took a final sip of the sweet dessert wine her father had produced to go with the apple pie and cream. 'Tom takes everything in his stride. And it really hasn't made any difference. Apart from the fact that the extra salary comes in very useful.'

Felicity stood up. 'Let's take our coffee in the sitting room.'

'You ladies go along,' Geoffrey said. 'We'll join you later. I've got a rather nice vintage port that I'd like Edward to try.'

As Amanda pushed back her chair she was wishing her father would offer her a glass of vintage port. It would be much more fun to stay on at the table with the men but, for the sake of keeping the peace, she would comply with tradition and join the ladies. It was archaic, really! But once again she would toe the line. She'd behaved impeccably so far, apart from a bout of understandable histrionics in the kitchen, and she didn't want to blot her copybook at this stage in the weekend.

Sipping her coffee in the sitting room, she could hear snippets of conversation floating through from the dining room. She derived vicarious pleasure from the occasional bursts of laughter.

'The men seem to be enjoying themselves,' Yvonne said. 'More coffee, Sis?'

Amanda looked up, startled. It was years since Yvonne

had called her Sis. And nearly as long since she'd picked up the coffee-pot! Her elder sister had always studiously avoided any tasks that were remotely domestic. And, cosseted here in the bosom of the family, she hadn't needed to perform the tasks that most women picked up out of sheer necessity.

Amanda knew that her sister was a good doctor and that she gave one hundred per cent to her patients. But off duty she didn't have to lift a finger if she didn't choose to. She had all the comforts of home with none of the responsibilities.

But she didn't have Tom! And she didn't have the freedom to let her hair down whenever she felt like it—both metaphorically and literally.

Looking at her sister now, the coffee-pot poised in her hands, Amanda couldn't remember the last time she'd seen her fair hair draped around her shoulders. It was always imprisoned at the back of her neck. But she was kind-hearted and her face, when she smiled as she was doing now, could be quite attractive in a studious sort of way.

'No more coffee for me, Yvonne. I'm going to turn in soon.'

'You must be tired, dear,' her mother said as she pecked her on the cheek. 'Your room's all ready.'

She went across to the dining room and stood in the doorway reviewing the scene. Her father was pouring out more port from the cut-glass decanter in the centre of the table.

'I'm going to bed. Goodnight, Daddy.' She dropped a kiss on the top of her father's bald patch in the way she'd done as a child, when his hair had first started to disappear.

Her father looked up and smiled. 'Goodnight, Amanda.'

He turned back to lean across the table towards Edward. 'As I was saying...'

Sitting by the window in her bedroom, she looked out at the night sky. The sun had set while they'd been having supper but the velvet darkness still retained some of the heat of the day. High above the hills across the valley the moon was shining down on the peaceful countryside. Nothing had changed since she used to sneak out of bed and huddle here on the window-seat, wrapped in her duvet, clutching the battered teddy that someone had put on the top of her bed. She hadn't seen it for years, but someone had obviously dug it out of the attic and put it there.

Would her mother have made such a nostalgic gesture? Most unlikely! It was probably Mrs Brown who'd known her since she was a child and was a kind, motherly soul.

Well, at least she wasn't entirely alone! But cuddling a teddy bear wasn't quite the same as... She pulled her knees up to her chin and sighed as she remembered Edward's kiss as they had embraced in the heathery hollow. She felt restless and not in the least bit tired any more. The fact that Edward was here in the house was too disturbing.

She was thirty years old and behaving like a dutiful child! She ought to march downstairs, throw open the dining-room door and tell Edward that she wanted him to come upstairs to her room. She needed to see him...but why? She'd managed her life for years without a man. Did she really want to get romantically involved with him? Because once she unleashed the emotions that she was trying to ignore there would be no going back!

A quick walk in the garden is what you need, she told herself sternly. Expend a bit of energy, get a breath of fresh air and when you get back to bed you'll go out like a light. She tied the cord of her cotton dressing gown in a firm knot and pulled on the ancient slippers that lived at the bottom of the wardrobe.

They might be ancient but they were still in excellent condition due to the fact that she'd hardly worn them over the last twelve years. Her mother had insisted she needed a new pair to take with her to medical school.

Outside, the smell of the roses was so refreshing. She crossed the lawn, feeling the dampness of the dew seeping into the thin soles of her slippers. She'd tiptoed down the back stairs and she was sure no one had seen her.

'Couldn't you sleep?'

She turned at the sound of Edward's voice. 'Where did you spring from?'

He gave a low, throaty laugh. 'I was finally able to convince your father that I didn't want another glass of port. And then I saw you sneaking out through the back door and decided I wouldn't be able to sleep either.'

She moved closer as if in a dream. The sensations she felt were as if she were sleepwalking. This sort of thing only happened in romantic films: meeting up with the man of your dreams in the middle of a rose garden on a warm, moonlit summer night. She admitted to herself that she hadn't planned this, but she'd hoped! Had she lingered just a few seconds longer than necessary at the back of the house when she'd noticed that the dining-room door was opening?

He was reaching out towards her and she sighed as she moved into his arms. He kissed her tenderly on the lips, his hands caressing her until her reawakened body was crying out for fulfilment. He was pulling aside the thin cotton gown, his fingers teasing and tantalising the hardening nipples of her breasts.

'Come back to my room,' he whispered, his gravelly voice husky with the promise of fulfilment.

She tensed as reality hit her. Her lips moved, automatically primed by years of abstinence. 'I can't. Not here where my parents—'

'You're a grown woman, Amanda. You've earned the freedom to do as you like.'

He was still holding her but she sensed that rationalising the situation was breaking the romantic spell for Edward as well as for herself.

'Edward, I can't change the way I feel about being here at home. If we were in another place…'

In the moonlight, she could see he was smiling down at her, waiting expectantly for her to finish her sentence. 'Are you about to make a promise?'

She drew in her breath. 'I mustn't make promises I can't fulfil.'

He put his arm round her shoulder and began to lead her back towards the house.

'One step at a time,' he whispered.

He opened the door for her and then stepped back, giving a brief wave as he walked away in the direction of the old stable block. She watched him go, her emotions churning away madly as she resisted the temptation to run after him.

One step at a time, he'd said. So was there a future together for them, in spite of the fact that she found she couldn't help holding herself back at the last minute and Edward, although wonderfully, tenderly passionate, had insisted that he didn't want to make another commitment for the rest of his life?

She sighed as she walked over to the stairs and went slowly up to her lonely bedroom.

But she had wonderful dreams! Her encounter in the rose garden with Edward had heightened her emotions and in her dreams he lifted her up and carried her away with him. She could even smell the evening dew on the grass.

He was carrying her up the stone stairs to his room over
the stables. She was clinging to him, her arms around his
neck, her lips against his warm skin... And then she
woke up to find she was almost strangling her poor teddy
bear! The sun was shining in through the window that
she'd left open so she could watch the moon. Sleep had
been a long time coming but she felt refreshed now as
she prepared to face Edward and the family at breakfast.

Family breakfast proved to be less of an ordeal than
Amanda had expected. Her father didn't appear any the
worse for over-indulging with the port and was more
lively and forthcoming than she'd ever known him.

'Next time, bring young Tom,' he called as Amanda
climbed into the car.

'I will.' She turned to wave to her mother and sister.

'So how on earth did you win my father round so
quickly?' she asked as soon as Edward had pulled the car
out into the main road. The sense of relief that they'd
survived the weekend under constant scrutiny had given
her a heady feeling of unreality.

Edward laughed. 'It was all basic psychology, really.
Get your patient to talk about the subjects they most enjoy
and steer them away from concepts that cause them pain.
So I didn't allow your father to dwell on the incidents in
the past that annoyed him. I started off by asking what,
in his experienced opinion, he thought about recent de-
velopments in cancer treatment and then we progressed
to—'

'So you talked shop even when you had your session
with the vintage port?'

'Ah, the conversation became less erudite after your
father's third glass. But by this stage he was in a benev-
olent mood and we were like old friends.'

She pulled the knot on her headscarf tighter as the car

gathered speed. 'I've noticed you're allowed to call him Geoffrey. Very few younger colleagues have been allowed to do that.'

He put his hand across her lap and squeezed her fingers. 'He actually asked me to.'

'After the third glass of port?'

He grinned. 'The second, actually.'

She gave his hand an answering squeeze. If only this moment of contentment could last for ever. It was a wonderful feeling to know that her father had made his peace with Edward.

'So you're firm friends?'

He put both hands back on the wheel. 'So long as I play Mr Nice Guy and avoid anything controversial. But, what the heck? Your father's getting on a bit. He's not getting any younger and…' He broke off.

'Yes?' She waited for what might be a stirring revelation.

'He told me—after the third glass—that he'd always longed for a son to take over from him at the surgery as he'd taken over from his father. He said that he'd had high hopes for me when I'd worked with him. He'd spent extra time with me and for some reason he couldn't fathom he'd come to regard me as his natural successor.'

Amanda sat very still, feeling the cooling air currents blowing around her. 'That would explain why he was so vitriolic when you left, wouldn't it? Maybe you broke his heart—like I did.'

She leaned back against the seat feeling drained by the conflicting emotions she'd experienced during the weekend. Neither of them spoke for a few miles and she closed her eyes.

'It's great to be heading south,' she said as they turned onto the motorway. 'I can be myself again. And I'm longing to see Tom and hear all about his weekend.'

'Me too!'

She glanced at Edward but he was concentrating on overtaking a lorry that was holding up traffic in the middle lane. Tom had grown fond of Edward; her father had become reconciled with him. What was holding her back from making a clear emotional commitment to their relationship?

Was she still scared that she might be hurt in the process? Or was she afraid that, if commitment to each other was on the cards, her confirmed bachelor lover would run away from her?

Couldn't she simply settle for a light-hearted fling? It would be better than nothing. Much better than denying herself the pleasure of being with Edward. Why didn't she try it? Lots of girls did, nowadays. It didn't have to be all or nothing. She could go along with a fun relationship for as long as it lasted.

If Edward felt the same way as she did. But, oh, she didn't want to spoil what they had now! This easygoing relationship where they didn't have to plan any changes in the future. Where they could work and play together and...

'You're very quiet all of a sudden.'

'It's difficult to talk over the sound of the air currents around us.'

'Well, so long as you're not worrying about...'

'About what?'

'About us, about where we're going.'

She gave a light-hearted laugh. 'I thought we were going home.'

'Home and back to reality,' he said.

Or at least that was what she thought he said, because he hadn't raised his voice to cope with the sound of the traffic and the rushing wind.

CHAPTER SIX

AMANDA was sitting on the floor helping her little patient to build a house out of brightly coloured wooden bricks when Edward walked into her consulting room.

'Some people get all the cushy jobs,' he said, ruffling the little blond boy's hair.

'Ben and I are making a very complicated house, I'll have you know,' Amanda said with mock indignation. 'Would you like to carry on without me for a minute, Ben, whilst I talk to Mr Burrows?'

The little boy nodded as he leaned forward to grasp another brick in his plump, dimpled hands. 'Shall I put that brick on top of this one, Amanda?'

'Yes. That's very good, Ben.'

She stood up, brushing her hands over the skirt of her navy blue suit as she drew Edward to one side.

'Ben's mother is having a consultation with the child development people,' she said quietly. 'She brought him along because his teachers had noticed he was very quiet and withdrawn in the reception class at school. As far as I can see, nobody has ever played with him. He's an only child and his mother is one of those fashion plates who wouldn't dream of getting down on the floor with her son.'

'Unlike some mothers who even play football with their sons.'

She smiled. 'Only if they're pressurised into playing goalie because nobody else wants that boring position.'

He gave her a wry grin. 'And a very good goalie you

made, if I may say so. When shall we have another game? This weekend?'

'I expect we won't get much choice in the matter,' she said fondly as she reflected that their weekends were forming a pattern.

Her life had changed so much in the last month, since their weekend at the family home. Edward had spent a lot of time with her and Tom. It was almost as if he wanted to be part of her family—but remain outside it when he chose. He was always the one who turned up at a moment's notice, suggesting a picnic in Regent's Park, or in the countryside if they had time to drive out there. But what he did with the rest of his off-duty time, she still had no idea.

The romantic side of their relationship, the intense feelings she'd felt when they'd been together in the Yorkshire Dales, on the hill and in the rose garden, had never been resurrected. She suspected she'd put Edward off the idea of romance when she'd been so adamant about not going with him to his room over the stables. She remembered how her attraction towards him had been intense and powerful as he'd held her in his arms in the moonlight. It would have been such bliss to ignore all her inhibitions.

But for a number of reasons, ingrained in her for a long time, she hadn't been able to do that and now she was paying the price of not knowing how Edward felt about her—apart from the obvious fact that she was a friend he enjoyed being with.

'Where shall I put this one?' her little patient asked, holding up a red tile.

'That one goes on the roof, Ben. I'll be with you in a moment. Was there any particular reason for your visit, Edward, or is this a social call—coffee machine broken down?'

'Coffee machine's fine. On a social level, may I invite

myself round for supper if I bring Tom's favourite take-away?'

She smiled. 'You mean the chicken stir-fry with bean-sprouts and—'

'And all the trimmings…OK?'

'Tom would never forgive me if I said no.'

'That's settled, then.' He was glancing at his watch. 'And on a professional level, I thought you'd like to know that I'm working in Surgical Outpatients and there's a small boy I want you to meet again. Remember William Fairburn, the little boy we took care of when Accident and Emergency were overloaded with that school coach disaster a few weeks ago?'

'I certainly do. Provisional diagnosis was appendicitis until you suspected it might be a renal calculus. Did William actually have a stone in his kidney?'

'Yes, he did.' Edward paused. 'I may need some moral support from you. Sister Longman's on holiday and I'd prefer to have an experienced member of staff with me when…'

He broke off and glanced across at Ben who'd stopped playing and was listening in. 'Look, I haven't time to explain the rest of the case history at the moment. Come along as soon as you've finished here. William's due with me in half an hour.'

'I'll be there.'

She went back to her little patient and knelt down in front of the almost-completed house. 'That's excellent, Ben. Shall I help you finish the roof?'

She found herself worrying about young Ben as she left her consulting room. It was such a pity that a perfectly healthy child should have endured such a difficult child-hood.

Put in the care of elderly grandparents at an early age

because his mother said she couldn't cope, he was now being reclaimed by his mother who, assuming he was well out of nappies, still didn't have a clue how to keep him happy. Amanda had been one of the experienced professionals asked to help with the little patient. She'd observed him while they'd been playing and would make her report to the psychiatric consultant. In her opinion it wasn't the child who needed therapy, it was the mother!

Edward looked up and smiled when she went into his consulting room. 'William has just arrived, Sister. Come through to the examination room.'

Their little patient was lying on the couch, holding his mother's hand.

'They did a great job with William, Sister,' Mrs Fairburn said as soon as Amanda walked in. 'Everybody thought it was his appendix until Mr Burrows spotted it was a different kind of pain and carried out some tests on his waterworks. The laser treatment broke up the stone and then he was put on a new drug I'd never heard of. I used to be a nurse,' she added, by way of explanation.

Amanda smiled. 'I thought you might have been. So how's William's health been since he went home?'

The mother frowned. 'Not too good. During the routine investigations they discovered a malignant lump in his kidney. He's been having intensive radiotherapy and drug treatment. That's why we're here today—to see how successful it's been.'

Amanda looked across at Edward and saw the compassion in his expressive eyes. A cancer-related lump in the kidneys was definitely bad news.

'I'm afraid it looks as if we'll have to operate on William, Mrs Fairburn,' he began carefully.

'You can tell me all the details, Mr Burrows,' Mrs Fairburn said, biting her bottom lip apprehensively. 'You'll have to remove that kidney, won't you?'

'I'm afraid we will,' Edward said quietly. 'We have no option if we're to check the spread of the malignancy. In fact we'd like to admit him today and start making the pre-operative tests.'

Mrs Fairburn's moist eyes flickered. 'I'd like to stay with him.'

'Of course,' Amanda said quickly. She looked down at the little boy, remembering how brave he'd been when he'd first come into hospital. 'You don't mind coming back into hospital, do you, William?'

William's brow puckered thoughtfully. 'Can I play on the bouncy castle?'

'I'll take you there myself, whilst they're making up your bed on the ward,' Amanda said.

Watching young William's valiant efforts to jump up and down on the bouncy castle, Amanda thought how feeble he'd become in the few weeks since she'd last seen him. His legs were like matchsticks and his arms flailed about in frustration. Finally, he flopped down on the cushions beside her.

'I've had enough,' he said breathlessly, snuggling against her. 'Can I go to bed now?'

Amanda put her arm around the little boy. 'Of course you can, William. Your mummy's up there waiting for you. Shall I ask one of the nurses to take you there?'

'Can't you take me?'

She knew she had a lot of things to finish before the end of the afternoon, but another few minutes wouldn't be too much to spare for a brave little boy like William. She took his hand and began leading him out into the waiting room. As she passed the ever-popular kiddy kitchen, complete with toy cooker, mini microwave, fridge and cooking utensils, she caught sight of a small, familiar patient.

'Hello, David! I didn't know it was your day for Outpatients.'

She poked her head inside the toy kitchen and smiled at the little boy who'd had a prosthesis fitted after his leg had been amputated. It was some time since she'd changed his dressing. In fact the wound on his stump had healed completely the last time she'd seen him. Perhaps Clive wanted to have his prosthesis checked. In which case, Edward would be dealing with him today—

Since Clive had gone on holiday a week ago, Edward had been overseeing his patients. It was strange she hadn't noticed David's name on the computer this morning. She tried so hard not to have favourite patients but there were a few who always tore at her heartstrings. And plucky little David was certainly one of them.

'I'll come and have a chat as soon as I've taken William to his ward,' she told David.

Returning to the play area some time later, she was expecting that David would have gone in for his appointment with Edward. She was surprised to see he was still there, rolling out a sheet of pretend pastry made from Plasticine.

'I'm back, David. Where's your mother?'

The little boy glanced around him. 'She must be somewhere in the hospital, but I haven't seen her for ages. Perhaps she's having something to eat. I'm feeling hungry, Sister.'

Amanda felt the first pang of anxiety. It wasn't like the mature, dependable Mrs Shuttleworth to leave her son for a long time on his own.

'Let's go and have a look for your mum in the cafeteria,' she said quickly.

Going out through the door of the play area, she asked

the young nurse at the desk how long it was since she'd seen David's mother.

'Sorry, Sister, I've only just come on duty and the nurse I took over from said all the children had their mothers with them.'

It was down in the cafeteria that Amanda really began to get worried. Mrs Shuttleworth was a well-known customer, having spent hours waiting around for her son during his outpatient and inpatient time in the hospital, and no one had seen her that day.

After giving David the ham, cheese and tomato pizza he'd said was his favourite, which he'd promptly wolfed down as if he'd not seen food for days, she took her young patient along to Orthopaedic Outpatients. Edward, in charge of Clive's patients, was filing the last of his computer case histories.

'Was David due to be seen today?' she asked quietly, holding tightly to her little patient's hand.

Edward shook his head. 'He's not on my list. Hello, David. Is Mummy—?'

'Mummy's not here at the moment,' said Amanda. 'She left David in the play area and—'

'Well, let's have a look at you, David,' Edward said, quickly gathering that they had a problem on their hands. 'How do you like your new prosthesis?'

David grinned. 'It's better than the old one. Watch this!'

The little boy set off across the consulting room at a rapid pace, turning as he reached the door in a pirouette movement before finally flopping down in Edward's chair behind the desk.

'Fantastic!' Edward said. 'Tell you what, David, it looks as if I won't need to do anything to your leg today, so why don't you let Sister take you back to the play area for a bit longer?'

David's face was wreathed in smiles as he stood up and made for the door. 'Thanks, Mr Burrows!'

'Ask the nurse out there to keep an eye on David whilst we start our enquiries, Amanda,' Edward whispered.

An hour later, Reception had phoned through to Edward's consulting room to say that all enquiries about David's mother had drawn a blank. Mrs Shuttleworth lived on her own with David, keeping herself very much to herself, according to the neighbours, who hadn't seen her all day. Someone thought Mrs Shuttleworth had a sister who sometimes visited but they didn't have an address.

So the police had been alerted and, after breaking into the house to ensure Mrs Shuttleworth wasn't there, they had now begun to search the surrounding area.

'We'll have to make provision with the social services for David to be cared for overnight,' Edward said to Amanda. 'More coffee?'

She shook her head. 'I'd better collect David from the play area. It's time for the nursing staff to go off duty. I'll take him to my room till we've sorted something out.'

Walking back with the little boy holding tightly to her hand, she knew it was going to be hard to hand him over to some unknown professionals. Back in her room, she picked up the phone and dialled Edward.

'What did social services say?'

'They're a bit stretched at the moment but they should be able to give us some help in the morning. The problem is that David's going to need specialist care because of his prosthesis so they asked if we could find a bed for him here at the hospital tonight. Orthopaedics haven't got a spare bed but they might be able to open up the new extension. He'd be on his own in there, of course, but the night staff would keep checking that—'

'No, I don't think so, Edward,' she said quickly.

The little eyes looking up at her with that heart-rending, frightened expression were alerting her to the fact that here was a boy who needed a lot of tender, loving care tonight. He'd gathered that his mother was missing. He was holding back the tears. And he wouldn't be happy to spend the night in a brand-new, smelling-of-cold-white-paint, six-bedded, empty room on his own.

'I'll take him home with me— Just until his mother turns up, which can't be long,' she added quickly as she felt the little boy squeezing her hand.

'You'll what? Amanda, you can't. You're not insured for—'

She cut the connection and smiled down at her patient.

His eyes were wide as he smiled back. 'Are you really going to take me home with you?'

'Would you like that?'

'Not 'alf! Have you got toys at your place?'

'I've got toys and a big boy for you to play with.'

'Amanda!' Edward rushed in through the door.

'Don't tell me—you've come to take our order for the Chinese take-away.'

Edward's frown gave way to a long, slow smile. 'You really are the absolute—'

'It will only be for a short time,' she said quietly. 'I know Mrs Shuttleworth. She won't—'

'Let's not speculate,' Edward said quickly. 'OK, you win.' He smiled down at David. 'Do you like Chinese food, David?'

'Not 'alf!' came the predictable reply.

David was cleaning the last of the chicken and rice from his plate with a large bread roll when Amanda's phone rang. Tom leapt up from the kitchen table but Edward got there first.

'Yes? Oh, thank God!'

Amanda was already at his side, trying to listen in.

'Thank you, Sergeant. No problem, we'll bring him along now.'

'Have they found my mum?'

Edward returned to the table and pulled the little boy onto his lap. 'Yes, they've found your mum. She's a little bit tired so she's going to take you to stay with her sister tonight.'

'And then will she go away again and leave me?'

'No, she's going to stay with you at your Aunty Dorothy's. Will you like that?'

'I'd rather we went home. Aunty Dorothy's a bit of a fusspot. Her house is sort of…well, it's too tidy. You know, you're not allowed to make a mess.'

Edward was smiling sympathetically as he lifted the little boy off his lap.

'Well, David, you see, the problem is that Mummy needs a rest for a few days and Aunty Dorothy's very kindly said she would be happy to look after both of you. So it seems to make sense to go along there, doesn't it?'

The little boy frowned as he thought about this. Eventually, he nodded. 'OK, if you think that's what Mum wants.'

Edward assured his little patient that it was exactly what his mother needed. 'As soon as Mummy's feeling better you'll be able to go home with her,' he added, as a carrot to the dejected but willing donkey.

'The police were marvellous!' Amanda said as they left the police station and climbed back into the car. 'They've had to file a report, of course, but they're not going to press charges. The case is in our hands now and, as we're only concerned with the welfare of the mother and child, that's how we'll handle it.'

'What did Mrs Shuttleworth tell you when you were having that quiet conversation?' Edward asked.

Amanda leaned back against the seat as she tried to remember the halting words that the distressed mother had spoken.

'She said she'd been fighting depression ever since her husband left her for a younger woman last year, and then, when her mother died a couple of months ago, everything seemed to get on top of her. Her sister, Dorothy, had told her she was going on holiday next week and she didn't think she could cope without any moral support at all, as she put it.'

Amanda shifted in her seat as she tried to remember the exact words of this deeply traumatised woman. 'This morning, she didn't know what she was planning to do when she left David in the play area. She said she knew he'd be safe there and someone would look after him. Apparently, she wandered around Regent's Park until the police found her and took her to the station, where she was eventually reunited with the sister they'd managed to track down.'

Edward nodded approvingly. 'This Aunty Dorothy seems like a good sort.'

Amanda was of the same opinion. 'Absolutely! She's cancelled her holiday and agreed to look after Mrs Shuttleworth while she's undergoing psychotherapy as an outpatient at the London Hospital.'

Edward slowed the car to a halt at the traffic lights. 'There's nothing like family when you're in a fix.'

She glanced sideways at Edward's determined profile. 'What about your family? Would they rally round if you were in a fix?'

She watched his fingers tighten on the wheel as he moved off again. He was staring straight ahead at the road. A thin drizzle of rain showed in the overhead street lights.

'What family? I was an only child.' He drew in his breath and remained silent for a few seconds.

Amanda tuned in to the steady rhythm of the windscreen wipers before she spoke again.

'But your parents...?'

'My parents were on an overloaded ferry which sank in the Philippines. There were no survivors.'

She could feel the hairs on the back of her neck standing up.

'How awful! I'm so sorry. I wouldn't have...'

Her voice trailed away as she realised the futility of trying to offer sympathy. However much you disagreed with your family on matters of principle, they were still family; they were still there even if they didn't offer you the kind of support you would have liked.

Edward was turning the car into her forecourt. Lights were shining from all the windows of the flats giving out a welcoming glow. Her mind was racing ahead. She would collect Tom from Alice's flat. How wonderful it was to have a son, her own flesh and blood. She was so lucky to have family—unlike Edward.

Her words of sympathy had seemed so trite but what else could you say in a situation like that? She was sorry she'd asked about Edward's parents. Still, it was one of the pieces of information she'd wanted to know about him. Anything she could glean about his background would help her to understand him better

She'd learned that, not only had he endured a disastrous marriage, but he'd lost both parents in a tragic accident. No wonder he sometimes built a shell around himself. He appeared totally self-sufficient for most of the time but she guessed that, deep down, he was emotionally vulnerable—like herself.

'Would you like to come in for a drink?' she asked quietly.

He hesitated. 'You're not too tired?'

She shook her head. 'I need to wind down after all the excitement.'

He switched off the engine and turned towards her, putting a finger under her chin so that she had to face him. 'I'd love to help you relax.'

She loved the sound of his deep, gravelly voice. It sent shivers of excitement down her spine. She couldn't think of anyone she would want to relax with at the end of a long day except Edward.

Her fingers entwined with his as they walked up the stairs. Alice had pushed a note under her door. 'Tom is sleeping in Mark's room tonight. See you in the morning.'

She started filling the kettle at the kitchen sink. Edward was standing behind her. He put his hands on her shoulders and his fingers clenched against the thin cotton of her blouse.

'I'd prefer a glass of wine.'

She put the kettle on the draining-board and swung round to face him. 'So would I. What wine have I got? You're the keeper of the wine cellar.'

It was Edward who always brought wine when he came to supper. Often he brought a spare bottle or two. He would jokingly tell her to put it in her wine cellar.

He was smiling as he selected a bottle of red wine from the small wooden wine rack on the kitchen dresser. 'Let's have something to conjure up warm sunny days by the sea; this wine from the Bordeaux region should be perfect. Loosely translated from the French, it says this is a vintage claret which will warm the heart and…'

She smiled, listening to his pseudo-French accent as she carried a couple of wineglasses through into the living room. Edward opened the bottle and sank down on the sofa beside her. She sipped her wine, finding that the deliciously warm, fruity taste was helping her relax.

'I'm glad you asked about my parents,' he said quietly after a few moments of calm relaxation. 'It's not something I usually like to talk about. But it's a good idea to get it out in the open.'

She turned her head and, seeing the anguished expression in his eyes, she remained silent. He was using her as a sounding-board, just as she'd used him all those years ago.

'I've come to terms with it,' he continued, half to himself. 'But, in a way, I blamed myself for what happened.'

She could feel her heart turning over as she listened to his anguished tone of voice. 'But why?'

He clenched the muscles of his jaw and she could see a nerve pulsing in his cheek.

'It was soon after I'd given up the idea of going into general practice,' he said, in a dull voice. 'My father was furious when I joined the travel firm. He told me it had been his dream—to have a son who was a respectable family doctor, someone that people looked up to. That was what had kept him going when he'd had to work long hours in a low-paid job at a textile factory in Bradford.'

He broke off and took a deep breath, as if to gather strength to continue his disturbing story.

'I wanted to show Dad that I wasn't a failure. I was able to buy air tickets at a discount price so I arranged that he and my mother should fly out to have a holiday with me in Singapore.'

He moved closer to her on the sofa and she held her breath as she waited for the doomed ending to his account. It was like watching the film version of the *Titanic*. The ending had been scripted even before the story started.

'I arranged for my parents to spend a week in the Philippines before they joined me in Singapore. They were so excited about this holiday of a lifetime, as my mother called it. They rang me from Manila when they arrived there…said they were having a wonderful time and they were looking forward to seeing me the following week…they'd planned a boat trip for the next day…'

She cupped her hands around his face and pressed her lips against his cheek in the way she would have soothed Tom if he'd been suffering from a nightmare. He turned and buried his head against her shoulder. She could feel that he was trembling. She held him close until the tremors subsided.

'You mustn't blame yourself, Edward. It wasn't your fault. You were trying to be kind and—'

He raised his head. 'I was trying to show off—to prove that I could make a successful life on my own terms. I wanted to do it my way. If only I hadn't bought those air tickets for them—'

'We mustn't look back and say if only, Edward,' she broke in. 'That's being wise after the event. We've both had to make difficult choices in our lives. We've neither of us taken the easy, predictable path.'

He gave her a long, slow, heart-rending smile. 'You're right. What did your father call us? The black sheep?'

Amanda smiled as the tension between them drained away. 'And he was right, wasn't he?'

'We've got a lot in common, you and I,' he said huskily.

When he took her in his arms, she felt a tremor of excitement. The deep emotions they'd shared that evening, both in their professional and private lives, had drawn them closer. She knew as soon as his lips closed over hers that she wouldn't fight against her feelings this time.

He began to caress her with gentle, tantalising hands, until, as her response deepened, she could feel the urgency of his desire matching her own. He drew her face close to his and looked into her eyes with a searching expression.

'I'd like to stay with you tonight, Amanda, if only to hold you in my arms all through the night. I know you've been traumatised by your experience with Mike and I recognise that it will take time to get over your frigidity but—'

'Frigidity?' She pulled herself away. 'Whatever gave you the impression I was frigid?'

'Sorry, frigidity is an emotive word. It's just the way you've come across on the occasions when I've tried to get closer to you. I was only going by what you'd told me of your early experiences with—'

'I merely told you that Mike had been totally unscrupulous. I didn't tell you…' She broke off. She'd hidden the facts even from herself for all these years.

He cradled her head against his shoulder. 'Go on, Amanda. It's a night for revelations. What didn't you tell me?'

'I didn't tell you that Mike forced himself upon me when I was recovering from the malaria, after he'd given me a sedative. I thought I was dreaming when I came round to find…'

She couldn't finish the awful description of her pain and humiliation.

'So you weren't in love with him?'

She shook her head. 'I thought I was when I first met him…I was only nineteen and he was the first man who'd awakened any desire in me. He said he wanted to marry me… Oh, he could be very charming when it suited him. This all took place during the weeks I was recovering from malaria, so marriage to the man who appeared to be curing my illness seemed an attractive idea. I was young, weakened by malaria, miles from my home and family…'

She pulled a wry face. 'But I was determined to wait until after we were married before we started a physical relationship. Apart from the conventional ideas instilled in me by my traditional parents, I was still physically very weak.'

She broke off, taking a deep breath to steady her nerves, experiencing once again the agony and doubt of that tumultuous period in her life as the memories flooded back.

'Take it easy,' Edward whispered. 'Don't go on if...'

She told him she was OK. It would help if he knew the true story.

'After Mike had forced himself on me, my feelings towards him changed. But he tried to convince me that it was because he loved me that he'd taken me like that. He said it was to find out if we were sexually compatible. And like the young fool that I was, I tried to believe him. But that was the only time we slept together.'

'And since your harrowing experience with Mike, have you had any other...?'

She bridled. 'That's a very personal question! For what it's worth, I haven't been able to contemplate the awful process of—'

'So you had become frigid?'

'No!'

Her denial made the moment seem all the more poignant as he scooped her up into his arms again.

'Amanda, don't you think it's time we settled this argument once and for all? If you'll put yourself in the hands of a kind, caring doctor who will promise not to frighten you in any way and—'

'Edward, I'm not in the least bit frightened. Frustrated, perhaps,' she said, revelling in the warm rush of liquid desire deep down inside her as she snuggled against him. 'I don't think I can wait much longer, so...'

He carried her across to the bedroom, pushing open the

door with his elbow, holding her so tightly against his chest that she could feel his heart beating through the cotton of his shirt. Her fingers seemed to have a mind of their own as she began to unbutton his shirt. She'd never thought herself capable of doing something so daring.

He lay down beside her on the bed, his hands smoothing back the ruffled hair from her forehead, his eyes tender with desire as he looked down at her enquiringly.

She could see that he still wasn't sure if she wanted him or if she was merely going through the motions to banish her old fear. He was so obviously afraid of hurting her.

'Edward…' She kissed him on the lips as she pulled him closer against her, revelling in the tremors of desire that were coursing through her body.

As he recognised that she was welcoming and responding to his caresses, his lovemaking became more urgent. She opened up to the waves of feeling sweeping over her, realising, with a sense of unreality, that they were both striving for the ultimate fulfilment. He teased, he tantalised, he made her feel that she was out of this world where reality had been replaced by pure sensation. And as she felt the sensations breaking over her entire body she cried out in ecstasy…

The morning sun was peeping over the window sill. She became aware that she wasn't alone in her warm, snuggly bed. Fluffy had advanced through the half-open bedroom door and settled herself on top of the duvet, purring like a motorbike engine.

Edward rolled onto his back, still half asleep, his eyes closed as he pushed back the duvet with one of his long, muscular legs. She caught a glimpse of his tanned, athletic body and felt a quiver of excitement at the memory of their lovemaking.

He rolled over and opened his eyes, his mouth curving into a long, lazy smile as he saw her.

Reaching out with both arms, he pulled her against him. 'I take it all back. I think we can definitely say, I was wrong. You weren't frigid.'

She smiled. 'Let's say you performed a miraculous cure last night, Doctor. Eleven years is a long time to wonder if you'll ever feel normal again.'

Her bedside phone was ringing. Fluffy sprang towards it and placed one paw on the handset. If Amanda didn't answer it immediately the cat would knock it off its cradle.

She groaned as she picked up the receiver. Reality was setting in again.

'Thank goodness it's you, Alice. I thought it might be the hospital. Is Tom OK?'

'He's fine. He's having breakfast with Mark in the kitchen. I thought I'd better keep him as long as I could.'

'That was very kind of you, Alice,' Amanda said carefully. 'I slept late this morning but I'll be up and about in—'

'I saw Edward's car on the forecourt when I looked out of the window this morning so…'

'Ah, so you jumped to conclusions?'

Alice giggled. 'Lucky girl!'

Edward was snuggling against her, stroking the skin at the nape of her neck. Fluffy had climbed onto Edward's back and was, jealously, trying to distract him.

'I'd better go, Alice. Give me ten minutes to—'

'You can have as long as you like because—'

'Ten minutes will be fine. And thanks, Alice.' She put down the phone and turned to look at Edward.

The expression in his eyes was definitely amorous. She would have liked to drown herself in those dark, mysterious pools of light where she could see her own reflection mirroring his newly awakened desire.

But there was work to be done—and she had to give some extra attention to her son. From now on she would have to be careful to share out her affection with the two men in her life.

Completely different kinds of affection for a son and for a lover. Was that how she now thought of Edward? And how long would he be her lover? As she extricated herself from his arms and began picking up the disarray of hastily discarded clothes from the floor, she knew she'd taken an irrevocable step.

But where was she going to go from here?

CHAPTER SEVEN

'MUM, we'll be fine on our own. Alice said we were old enough so…'

Amanda recognised that Tom was giving her the sort of look that was meant to imply that she was a dinosaur. She gathered up the cereal bowls from the kitchen table and dumped them in the sink. Raising her head, she looked out at the thin mist evaporating from the roof-tops. There was a definite autumnal feel about the morning even though it was still September. The rosy glow behind the block of flats to the east showed that the sun would eventually drag itself from its cloudy duvet up into the sky, but the long hot days of summer were definitely over.

'Shall we go and ask my mum again?' Mark was whispering to Tom.

Amanda swung round and regarded the two boys. Tom's hair needed cutting, she noticed. And it certainly needed washing! He looked like one of the sheep that cropped the grass in the field next to the Grayson surgery.

'Did you shower after swimming yesterday, Tom? Your hair looks—'

She was on her way back to continue clearing the table but she broke off as she tripped against something hard on the floor.

Tom rescued his satchel from the floor at the side of his chair. 'Sorry, Mum. There wasn't time for a shower so I just rubbed my hair on a towel. I had a football practice straight afterwards and then…then I forgot. Well, my hair got washed in the swimming baths, didn't it?'

Mark was standing up, his eyes registering the boredom

126

he felt at the way the conversation was turning. 'We're going to be late if we don't start walking now.'

'You're right.' Tom looked at his mother enquiringly. 'So…?'

She knew when she was beaten. She couldn't wrap her precious son in cotton wool for the rest of his life. He had to go out into the big wild world and become streetwise in every way. All the dangers of living in London threatened, but he would have to learn to cope with them. And she would have to learn how to cope with her fears for his safety.

'Take extra care at the traffic lights. If you hear an ambulance or a police car with its emergency horn sounding, remember that they will be rushing straight through the lights, so—'

'Mum, we've had lessons on safety at school,' Tom said plaintively. 'We're not babies, you know.'

He turned at the door and held his face up for a kiss. This was unusual under the circumstances, she thought as she pressed her cheek against his. When his friends were around he usually swaggered out with only a perfunctory call of goodbye.

She closed the door, returning to the table to sink down onto her chair and pour another cup of coffee from the cafetière. The phone began to ring as soon as she picked up her cup. It was too early for the hospital to be contacting her—or was it?

'Amanda Grayson here.'

'Wow, you sound high-powered this morning!'

She relaxed as she heard Alice's voice. 'The boys have just gone. Did you say Mark could walk to school by himself?'

'That's what I'm ringing about. Can I save the phone bill and come down for a chat? Have you time before you zoom off to your executive office?'

'Yes, do come down. I'm nearly ready. Are you feeling better? Mark said you had a headache and you'd asked him to go down and have breakfast with Tom.'

'I needed a bit of peace and quiet to think about... Well, anyway, thanks for feeding him and—'

'My pleasure. See you in a minute.' She put the phone down knowing that Alice had a tendency to ramble on a bit and, whilst she had time for a short chat, anything more would put her schedule right out.

She dashed into the bedroom and put the finishing touches to her outfit for the day: clean white blouse, newly dry-cleaned navy blue suit, brand new tights without holes.

'Help yourself to coffee, Alice,' she called as she heard the door closing and footsteps crossing into the kitchen.

'You look so smart!' Alice said as Amanda emerged from the bedroom.

'Boringly smart,' Amanda said. 'The same old uniform every day. Sometimes I wish I was one of these girls going off to an office in the city with a different outfit every day.'

Alice sighed as she pushed back her long dark hair. 'At least you do go out to work, whereas...' She spread her hands wide. 'What do I do?'

Amanda leaned forward across the table. 'You're always here when the boys need you, Alice, and you make it possible for me to go to work. I couldn't have done what I've done without you, Alice.'

Alice sighed, cradling the cup in her hands.

'It's been great for Mark to have another boy to grow up with. But they are growing up, our boys, and I'm beginning to dread feeling useless. They won't need me much longer. You know that I keep thinking that I ought to get myself a job...well, there was a job advertised in the evening paper: stacking shelves in the supermarket on the early shift. If you could have Mark for breakfast every day, the boys could walk to school by themselves and I'd be back before they came home from school, ready to give them some tea.'

The very thought of stacking shelves at the supermarket gave Amanda the creeps, but she didn't want to discourage Alice if that was what she wanted to do so she smiled encouragingly. Alice was capable of a much more prestigious job but she would have to start at the bottom.

'If you think you'll enjoy working at the supermarket, then go for it, Alice. It sounds a good arrangement.'

Alice put down her cup and leaned across the table. 'If Edward was staying here, would he mind you having an extra boy for breakfast?'

'He doesn't stay here unless Tom is sleeping upstairs at your place,' Amanda said quickly.

'Why not?'

Amanda drew in her breath. 'I wouldn't feel...er... comfortable sleeping with Edward if Tom was in the next room.'

And there was another reason. In the weeks since they'd become lovers she'd learned a great deal about Edward, and one of the things was that he was determined to keep his independence. He very rarely stayed over at her flat, preferring that she spend the night with him at his place in the Barbican whenever she could get away.

'On the rare occasions that Edward stays on here, it's always when Tom is upstairs spending the night at your place,' Amanda said carefully. 'And he always leaves very early in the morning. The reason he gives is that he wants to go back to his own apartment to check the post, or the answering machine or—'

Alice made an impatient clicking sound with her tongue. 'But that's all an excuse, isn't it? I mean, he's probably too early for the post...'

'Not if he hasn't been home the day before,' Amanda said, loyally sticking up for Edward even though Alice was voicing her own misgivings.

'Well, anyway, he could check his answering machine by ringing from his mobile or—'

'I know, I know.' She didn't want Alice to rub salt into her wounds. 'The point I'm making is that it's always perfectly OK for Mark to come down here for breakfast, so go ahead and apply for the job if you fancy it.'

Alice pulled a face. 'I don't really fancy stacking shelves but I've got to start somewhere. And I'll meet people.'

'You'll be promoted to manager before you know where you are,' Amanda said. 'You got good exam results at school, didn't you? Put all that down on your application form.'

'You know what the problem with Edward is, don't you, Amanda?'

'No, I don't, but I'm sure you're going to tell me.'

'Edward wants to have his cake and eat it. He wants to be part of a ready-made family: football in the park at weekends, picnics in the countryside, someone to take to the cinema and concerts. Are you happy with this arrangement? I mean...'

'Yes, it suits me fine.'

Amanda had tried to disguise her indignant feelings but failed miserably. Over the years she'd come to realise that Alice had a knack of hitting the nail fairly and squarely on the head. They'd become like sisters. They'd shared their problems with each other and come up with solutions.

But, she realised, with a heart-rending pang, her relationship with Edward was sacrosanct. It was too precious to discuss with anyone—anyone except Edward, that was. And she knew it was only a question of time before she told him that she didn't want to carry on like this for the rest of her life.

'I've got to go, Alice,' she said quickly.

Alice stood up. 'Me too. I'll go and phone the supermarket. They open early and they're interviewing today.'

'Good luck, Alice!'

'Thanks!'

The grey brickwork of St Elizabeth's Hospital loomed up in front of Amanda out of the mist. Hurrying through the glassed-in entry way, she crossed the mini shopping mall, passing a woman in a long coat holding a baby who was hurrying out of the building. Amanda waved to Mrs Lewis, who was adjusting her plastic apron at the front of her flower and fruit shop. Mrs Lewis smiled and waved back. 'Call in for some apples, Sister, on your way home. Young Tom will enjoy one of these and I've got more than I can handle.'

'Thanks a lot!'

What a kind woman Mrs Lewis was! She'd taken a real interest in Tom since the days when he'd been very small and Amanda had brought him with her and put him in the hospital crèche.

There was a note on her desk. Apparently, Edward wanted to see her as soon as she arrived. She tapped on his door and went inside.

He stood up, came round the desk and put his arms round her shoulders. She could smell his distinctive aftershave, which was only slightly masking the scent of the soap she'd sometimes used in his shower after a night of passionate lovemaking. Every nerve in her body seemed to stir, to become finely tuned towards his excitingly virile body, but she remembered that they were in a work situation and she couldn't afford to get carried away so early in the day.

She allowed him to kiss her on the lips, savouring the exciting texture of his mouth, but pulled herself away quickly.

He raised one dark eyebrow as he looked down at her. 'Do I sense a certain cooling of the atmosphere, today? Is it the onset of autumn, the prospect of the colder weather or…?'

She tried to make light of her mood as the thought crossed her mind that if they were having a real relationship, recognised by everyone as a couple, they wouldn't have to snatch these precious, delicious moments. And she wouldn't suffer the frustration she felt when they hadn't been able to get together for a few days.

'I've simply got work to do, that's all,' she began. 'So if—'

'Your sister phoned me.'

She stared at him. 'Yvonne phoned here?'

'This morning.' He went back behind his desk. 'She's in London for a GP conference and she wants us to meet her for lunch today.'

'But why didn't she phone me at home?'

'Does Yvonne often phone you at home?'

Amanda sank down on a chair at the other side of Edward's desk and gave him a wry smile. 'In all the years I've been living in London she's never phoned me.'

'Exactly! I think she wants a third party to be there when she gives you her news.'

Amanda frowned. 'What news?'

Edward shrugged. 'Search me. She simply said she'd like me to be there when she told you some news. She wants us to meet her in Regent's Park at one o'clock. She's going to bring sandwiches from Marks & Spencer and she's described exactly which seat near the lake where we—'

Amanda couldn't help laughing. 'It's all so cloak and

dagger! But it's just like Yvonne! She always did have a sense of the melodramatic. Anyone else meeting up with their sister would book a table at a restaurant or at least go for a pizza.'

Edward smiled. 'Perhaps she wants to feed the ducks, or fill her lungs with the precious fresh air of London before she returns to the frozen north.'

'Whatever can her news be about? And why can't she give it over the phone?'

'You'll have to contain your curiosity during the morning. You're working in Ophthalmics, aren't you?'

Amanda nodded. 'Sister Helen Crowther is on a course in advanced ophthalmics, so that's where I'll be if you need me.'

He gave her a rakish grin. 'I always need you, Amanda.'

She sidestepped his advances and made for the door, but before she reached it one of the early shift nurses came in rapidly after the briefest of knocks. The open door revealed a distraught mother being comforted by another nurse, and, on demanding to know the problem, Amanda and Edward soon realised they had one of their worst nightmares on their hands—baby Charlotte Jackson had been taken by a bogus nurse. Almost before they had time to assimilate that news, the phone rang.

Edward snatched up the receiver, and barked, 'Yes?' He listened, murmured, 'Thank God!' in heartfelt tones, before saying, 'Thanks, Ross. Keep me informed.'

He moved towards Mrs Jackson and, taking her hands, he persuaded her to listen to him. 'Mrs Jackson, I've just heard that Dr Webster, a doctor from the neurology department, spotted Charlotte being taken, and is in hot pursuit in a taxi. The police have been alerted, and I'm sure we'll get Charlotte back very soon. Will you let Sister

Grayson take you for a cup of tea, and I promise we'll let you know exactly what is going on at all times?'

Gulping valiantly, Mrs Jackson clutched his hands, but was obviously reassured by his calm and gentle manner, and Amanda, after a speaking look at Edward, put her arm around Mrs Jackson and led her into her office. The next fifteen minutes seemed the longest of their lives, until Edward came back to them, smiling delightedly. 'The baby is safe, Dr. Webster has her, and the police are bringing them back to us immediately. I know you want to see Charlotte immediately, Mrs Jackson, but would you wait with Sister Grayson, and I'll go and meet them in the foyer? After I've checked Charlotte over, I'll bring her back to you.'

When all the necessary procedures had been followed, and Outpatients was once more quietly bustling, Amanda finally made it to the ophthalmics clinic.

Ophthalmics was a fascinating department, but some of the techniques were rather complicated and it was a couple of years since she'd worked there full-time.

Her first patient was a dear little baby girl who'd had an operation to have cataracts removed from both eyes. George Pearson, the ophthalmic consultant, was trying, unsuccessfully, to examine the eyes while little Fiona squirmed and struggled on the examination couch.

'I think we'll have more success if I hold Fiona in my arms,' Amanda said quietly.

George Pearson was an experienced consultant, nearing retirement age, and he didn't take kindly to being told how to do his job.

He drew in his breath and frowned. 'Fiona's always been a difficult baby. The only time she's conformed is when I've had her under an anaesthetic.'

'She's only twelve weeks,' Amanda said soothingly as she cradled the baby girl against her white cotton blouse.

Looking down at the trusting blue eyes, she thought how wonderful it would be to have a baby again—a little sister for Tom. She'd never thought like that before. Tom had been a one-off, her only child, and likely to stay that way. But now, her life had changed dramatically and…

'Move Fiona's head to the side, Sister…that's fine, now hold it still.'

Mr Pearson was smiling and nodding as he looked through his ophthalmoscope. 'Splendid!' He raised his hand and twirled it above the baby's head. She followed it, turning her head to watch his antics.

'It's miraculous!' Amanda said. 'Restoring her sight when she was almost blind at birth.'

The consultant pushed back his chair and stood up. 'Before modern technology she would have gone through life being partially sighted. Would you like to take Fiona back to her mother and bring the next patient in, Sister?'

Amanda wrapped a thin blanket around the baby and walked slowly out of the consulting room. That indefinable smell of a baby's skin, the talcum powder and soap, was tantalising her nostrils. Fiona gurgled and smiled as she reached out her dimpled hands towards Amanda.

'Fiona's mother's gone for a cup of tea, Sister,' the staff nurse on duty in the waiting room told her. 'Shall I look after her until…?'

'No, that's all right, Staff Nurse. I'll wait with her. Would you take the next patient in to Mr Pearson?'

'You're a beautiful girl, Fiona,' Amanda whispered, settling herself on a waiting-room chair as soon as the staff nurse had departed. 'I wish I had a baby just like you.'

She took a deep breath, telling herself to stop being so soppy! She was a professional, used to dealing with babies in her daily life. Besides, babies weren't all magic. Far from it!

She tried to remember the difficult part of Tom's babyhood. The broken nights under the mosquito net in Africa when she'd been all alone with her baby, and thousands of miles from her family. She'd been forced to give up her job at the charity relief centre towards the end of her pregnancy and had been urged to go home to England. But she'd insisted on staying, convinced that once she'd recovered from having her baby she would be able to resume her work, taking the baby with her like the African mothers did.

But it hadn't been as easy as she'd envisaged, and she'd realised this was no sort of life for her child. She'd reluctantly come to the conclusion that she would have to go back to England and get herself some medical qualifications so that she could give Tom a decent education and upbringing.

But she realised now, with a pang of excitement, that if she were to have a baby here in England, with the good salary she was earning, life would be wonderful. She could really enjoy this one. Every little moment as the baby changed rapidly from foetus in her womb to real live person. But it would have to have a father—not just any father. The most wonderful father in the world who...

'Sorry I was so long, Sister.' Fiona's mother was tapping her on the shoulder. 'Are you OK? You seemed miles away when—'

Amanda smiled. 'I'm fine.' She handed over the baby. 'I was enjoying holding little Fiona. She's gorgeous!'

'We think so! Thanks, Sister.'

Hurrying back to Mr Pearson's consulting room, she found that the staff nurse was helping him with a little boy who'd undergone recent surgery for a detachment of the retina.

'You can see where I sewed back the retina, which is like a piece of net curtain stretched across the back of the eye,' the consultant was explaining. 'It acts rather like a camera to catch the images that are thrown onto it and, obviously, if it becomes detached the patient can't see.'

Mr Pearson raised his head to look at Amanda. 'Staff Nurse has asked if she can stay and help me for the rest of the morning. She wants to specialise in ophthalmics, so supervising the waiting room isn't going to give her much experience.'

'Of course she can. I'll redeploy someone to take over out there.'

Having accomplished the necessary staff change, Amanda was more than relieved to get back to her office so that she could get her administration schedule organised.

She enjoyed the hands-on nursing but there was always the steady drip drip drip of paper and computer work. If she was honest, the hands-on work was infinitely preferable to staring at a flashing screen, but she'd known what she'd been taking on when she'd applied for this job. And she was lucky to have been selected.

She'd come a long way since she'd worked in the hot African sun for a minimal wage!

Her phone rang as she was swiping her lipstick across her mouth, in an attempt to make herself look presentable for the meeting with her sister. Got to keep the flag flying and show that she could still make an effort even on a working day.

She hurried over to the phone. 'Oh, it's you, Edward. I thought it might be Yvonne, to say she couldn't meet us.'

'Do I detect a spot of wishful thinking?'

She laughed. 'Well, I must admit I'm not looking forward to sandwiches in the park with my sister.'

'It's a lovely day out there now. I thought it would be

nice to walk round rather than taking the car and having all the hassle of finding a parking space, so we'd better leave soon.'

'Give me two minutes to repair the damage, Edward.'

She put down the phone and returned to scrutinise her reflection in the mirror. She dabbed some powder over her nose.

She felt a shiver of apprehension. Whatever was Yvonne going to reveal?

Some dark secret about the family? Skeletons pulled out of the family closet? After the experiences she'd had during her thirty years, nothing could surprise her!

CHAPTER EIGHT

AMANDA noticed that the morning mist had completely disappeared as she hurried beside Edward through the park. As they passed the tennis courts, where they could hear the hard thwack of ball against racket, Edward paused for a moment to consult the piece of paper on which he'd written the instructions that Yvonne had given him over the phone.

'As soon as we reach the lake, we have to turn right...'

He started walking again and Amanda increased her pace to keep up with Edward's long legs.

She could see the sun shining on the lake. Mothers and children were enjoying the late September sunshine. Toy boats bobbed on the water, some of them steered by their excited owners from the edge of the lake as they zapped on their electronic remote controls. Perhaps Yvonne's idea of a picnic in the park wasn't such a bad idea after all! But what on earth was her elder sister up to? It was all so mysterious!

'There she is!' Edward said and, taking hold of Amanda's hand, he led her towards the seat where her sister was sitting.

Yvonne looked up and gave a nervous, somewhat sheepish, entirely out-of-character smile. Usually, she was brimming with self-confidence, ready to take exception to ideas that Amanda put forward, almost as a matter of principle or sheer bloody-mindedness. But today...

Amanda felt self-conscious as she advanced towards the seat, Edward holding tightly to her hand. The first thing she noticed was that Yvonne had been to the hairdresser and had her long, fair hair, usually banished in a knot, cut to a medium length that made an attractive frame around her face. It even looked as if she'd treated herself to a soft perm. What an incredible transformation! But she wouldn't dare to remark on it unless her sister brought up the subject.

'Hello, Yvonne. Have you been waiting long?'

Best to start out with a banal question, Amanda thought as she sat down beside her sister.

'About seven minutes, actually.'

True to type—always very precise in her calculations. Yvonne would have been eyeing her watch and ignoring the pleasant outdoor scenery. Amanda cleared her throat. 'Well, this is a pleasant surprise, meeting up with you like this. What was it that—?'

'Would you like a sandwich?' Yvonne said quickly, fishing inside a shopping bag. 'There's ham, chicken, egg and cress—or shall we share them out?'

'Let's share,' Edward said, trying to ease the proceedings.

'And I've got some small bottles of spring water,' Yvonne said, delving into the bottom of the bag.

'How lovely! Thanks,' Amanda said as she held out her hand. 'What a great day for a picnic!'

Her eyes met Edward's and she saw that he was on the point of laughing at her attempt to cut through the tension. She gave him a mock frown, willing him not to make any facetious remarks.

Swallowing a piece of chicken sandwich, she tried again to elicit some information from her sister.

'I can't stay long, Yvonne. What was it that—?'

'I haven't much time either,' her sister cut in defensively. 'There's a medical seminar I'm expected to attend at two-thirty. I wanted to meet you here on neutral ground, so to speak…'

'I don't quite follow,' Amanda said cautiously. 'Much as I'm enjoying the lovely sandwiches, I had wondered why—'

'What I have to say is in complete confidence. I couldn't risk any of my colleagues walking into a restaurant and overhearing...'

'Why don't you put Amanda in the picture, Yvonne?' Edward said evenly. 'We're all busy professional people and—'

'First, I've got to ask you not to breathe a word to Mum and Dad.'

'Yvonne, I'll sign the Official Secrets Act if you'll just spill the beans!'

Looking up at Edward, Amanda could see his lip trembling as he tried to hold back his laughter. Well, she'd enjoyed coming out with that phrase she'd heard gangsters use in black and white mystery films. And she felt as if she were taking part in a film at the moment!

The whole scenario was reminiscent of how she imagined MI5 would operate! It was as if at any minute a spy would pop up behind the seat, grab her chicken sandwich and extricate the coded message hidden inside it...

Yvonne was carefully folding and refolding one of the plastic wrappers. 'It's not easy for me to tell you this, Amanda.'

Edward took hold of Amanda's hand and squeezed it as he leaned across her to speak to her sister.

'Just try to get the words out, Yvonne,' he said, barely concealing his laughing impatience. 'Amanda and I have to get back to Outpatients otherwise—'

'I've got a dark secret. I've never told anyone before. I'm not proud of what I've done and I need some moral support if...if it becomes public knowledge.'

Yvonne paused. Amanda stared at her sister. 'What have...?'

'I've been having an affair for the past five years with the husband of a patient.'

An affair! Her sister! Her jolly-hockey-sticks sister who'd never had a boyfriend in her life—or so Amanda had thought.

'With the husband of a patient?' Edward queried evenly. 'He wasn't your patient, was he?'

'Only at the beginning. Before…before we went to bed together.' Yvonne's face had turned bright red with the effort of this admission. 'When we decided that we were going to take our relationship one step further I asked Trevor to sign up with another practice.'

Edward gave an audible sigh of relief. 'Very wise. So what's the problem? Has the wife found out?'

Yvonne cleared her throat nervously. 'Trevor's wife died last year. She'd been suffering from motor neurone disease for the past ten years. Trevor nursed her at home with the help of the community nurses as long as he could. For the last two years of her life she was in a nursing home.'

She lowered her voice, her eyes staring out across the blue stretch of water. 'She didn't know about us. We didn't cause her any pain by…by being together but I know we'll be blamed for…'

She broke off as her voice cracked and she seemed unable to go on with her startling confession.

Amanda was still reeling from the thought of her sister actually having a sexual relationship with a man. They'd never discussed sex together as she imagined most sisters would do. It had been a taboo subject and she'd been completely in the dark where Yvonne was concerned. She'd always thought that she was probably a virgin and likely to stay that way for the whole of her life.

'But if Trevor's wife has died, and she didn't know about your affair, what's the problem?' she asked quietly.

'The problem is that I'm pregnant and I don't know how Trevor will take it.'

'Haven't you told him?' Edward asked, his voice showing his surprise that anyone should want to withhold such an important piece of information.

Amanda was still reeling with the shock of the announcement and felt as if she had been struck dumb.

'I don't know how he's going to take it,' Yvonne said. 'He's a lot older than me. He's got a grown family already and I don't think he'll want to start again...in which case I'll be on my own...like you, Amanda,' she added sheepishly.

She broke off and Amanda sensed that tears weren't far away.

'That's why I wanted to talk to you today, Amanda. You've brought up a child on your own. Do you think I'll be able to cope? I'm dreading our parents' reaction. I'm going to need your moral support when I have to break the news. Can I count on you to be there when I need you?'

Amanda swallowed hard. She could have done with some moral support herself when Tom had been small but it hadn't been forthcoming. She'd met with a wall of silence from her sister when she'd first visited the family home.

'I know I've no right to expect you to stand by me, Amanda. That's why I asked Edward to be here with us...in case you turned against me. I'm sorry for the way I reacted when you came back from Africa with Tom. I had no right to take sides with our parents like that and—'

'Of course, I'll stand by you. I wouldn't want you to go through...'

Amanda broke off, not wanting to worry her sister about the months ahead. It was enough that she could at last feel reconciled with her. It had taken another crisis to effect their reconciliation and for the first time in her life she felt a close sisterly bond between them.

'Don't you think you ought to tell Trevor you're expecting his child?' Edward put in quietly. 'I think you may find him more sympathetic than you imagine. It must be a wonderful experience having a baby with someone you love.'

Now it was Amanda's turn to feel the prickling of tears behind her eyes. Listening to Edward's deep, gravelly voice expounding the joys of parenthood made her want to cry with relief.

Was he speaking objectively, in terms of other people having babies, or was it remotely possible that he might have a secret wish for a family himself? She'd seen the way he treated their small patients with such skill and tenderness. He'd make a perfect father. But he'd have to renounce his single status first and he probably wasn't sure if he could do that.

'This was the advice I wanted you to give,' Yvonne said slowly. 'Do you think I should tell him?'

'Of course you should tell him!' Amanda put in forcefully. She'd never thought of her sister as a ditherer before. Yvonne had always been strong, forceful, no-nonsense, bite on the bullet and get it over with. Maybe it was the disturbance to her hormones that was making Yvonne react as she was doing now.

Amanda had saved the crusts from her sandwich and now tossed them out over the path. A couple of sparrows alighted in front of her and began hoovering up the remains.

Edward stood up. 'We've got to go now, Yvonne. You've got my telephone number if you need any more help—or just a chat.' He smiled sympathetically.

Amanda leaned across and kissed her sister's cheek. 'Don't worry. It always seems darkest before the dawn.

This time next year it will all have worked itself out. You'll be so wrapped up in being a mother—that is unless you're contemplating a termination...?'

'Never! This baby was conceived in love so...'

'Go for it!' Amanda said. 'And ignore any adverse comments. That was the first thing I had to learn so that I could survive. Just close your ears and walk away if the criticism gets too much for you. Remember, our grandmother always used to say, sticks and stones may hurt your bones but words can't touch you.'

Yvonne put out her hand and squeezed her sister's. 'Thanks, Amanda. You've been great. I'll be in touch and tell you how I get on.'

Edward followed Amanda into her consulting room and walked across to the coffee-making machine. 'I need a caffeine jag before I start work. I'm in theatre at three, and likely to be there for a few hours. Would you like a cup?'

'"Not 'alf!" as young David would say. He's coming in this afternoon to have a replacement prosthesis fitted. He's outgrown the last one.'

'So you're working with Clive, are you?'

'Only for the last few patients. I've got to finish this paperwork first.' She took the cup that Edward was holding out towards her. 'Thanks, I need something to put me back in a working mood. I just can't believe what Yvonne told us. She's always been this strait-laced, butter-wouldn't-melt-in-her-mouth type of person.'

Edward leaned against her desk while he sipped his coffee. He was too close for comfort. Too close for Amanda to begin thinking about work!

'And correct me if I'm wrong, but hasn't Yvonne always been the apple of her father's eye?'

'Oh, absolutely! No question about it, Yvonne's news

will... I was going to say kill him, but I'll stop being so melodramatic. Let's say that my father will react unfavourably, but, if she follows my advice and doesn't take it too much to heart, she'll survive. I did.'

He leaned forward and kissed the tip of her nose. 'Shall we invite Yvonne to join the black sheep club?'

Amanda laughed. 'We could consider her membership. But she's got to show she can survive under adverse conditions like we did. How do you think she'll cope when the going gets tough? I can't even imagine her changing a nappy. She always used to call for a nurse if there was anything messy to be done in the surgery.'

Edward placed his cup on the desk and put his arms around her. 'I think, deep down, she's probably as tough as her little sister.'

His voice was husky. She looked up into his eyes and saw real tenderness. 'Mmm, I'd like to stay here like this all afternoon,' she whispered, half to herself.

He kissed her long and hard on the lips. She felt herself melting against him, all her responses triggered by the feel of that familiar, loved and desired muscular body. She already felt married to him in all but name and living situation.

He pulled himself away and looked down at her, longingly. 'Hang onto that feeling until this evening. My place or yours?'

She hesitated. Would playing hard to get make him realise that he couldn't continue to have his cake and eat it, as Alice had put it this morning so succinctly? It might do, but on the other hand it could have completely the opposite effect. Edward was a very independent person and he might not want her to start dictating the terms of their relationship.

'Come round to mine,' she said quietly. 'Alice has in-

vited Tom to spend the night with Mark. They're working
on a school project together, and, Edward…'

'Yes?' He turned at the door and looked enquiringly at
her.

She took a deep breath. She wanted to suggest that he
stay for an early breakfast but at the last moment she
chickened out.

'What time will you arrive?' she heard herself saying.
'I'll cook something.'

'As soon as I can get away from theatre. About eight,
I expect.'

She timed her administration work so that she would be
available to help out in Orthopaedics Outpatients when
young David was due to arrive. Going into Clive's consulting room, she was pleased to see that David's mother
was looking much better than the last time she'd seen her.

She smiled. 'It's good to see you again. How are you?'

Mrs Shuttleworth smiled. 'I'm fine! Thanks for all your
help, Sister, when…when I was going through a bad
time.'

'Your sister was very helpful,' Amanda said quickly.

'Yes, we're very close. There's nothing like family in
a crisis, is there?'

'I agree!' Amanda said wholeheartedly.

Clive cleared his throat, impatient to get on with his
examination of young David, who was reading a comic
as he lay stretched out on the couch.

Amanda undid the wrapping round the new prosthesis
and measured David's leg against it to check that he
hadn't grown since the latest measurements had been
taken.

'This is going to be a superleg, David,' she told her
patient as she and Clive fixed the prosthesis in position.

'Can I try it?' David couldn't wait to climb off the

couch and put both feet on the ground. 'Yeah! I like it. Can I try kicking a football with it?'

'You'll have to ask your physiotherapist to help you with that,' Amanda said quickly. 'See what she says when you have your next session.'

At the end of the afternoon, Amanda asked Clive if he was satisfied with the staff situation now that she and Edward had made new arrangements for his department.

'I'll be glad when Julia gets back from her extended maternity leave,' he said dryly.

'But the temporary sister is pulling her weight, isn't she? Edward chose her from a list of well-qualified nurses at the agency.'

'She's not as good as Julia. Why she had to go and get herself pregnant, I'll never know!' He switched off his computer and swivelled round in his chair to look at Amanda who was stacking the sheets from the examination couch.

'I expect her husband had something to do with it,' Amanda said wryly. 'And they'd been trying for a baby for years.'

'Well, Julia certainly hit the jackpot this time with triplets.'

Amanda smiled. 'That's why she was so ill at the beginning. It was a bit of a shock to her body.'

Clive shrugged. 'I shouldn't have given her all that time off to go to the fertility clinic. And now you and Edward have completely spoiled her by giving her the rest of her pregnancy off and the first three months after the birth as well.'

Amanda pulled a chair up to the side of Clive's desk. 'Oh, come on, Clive, give the poor girl a chance! How would you like to produce triplets and then rush back to work for a constantly complaining boss? It's only because her mother and sister have offered to look after the triplets that she'll be able to get back at all.'

He stared at her, his eyes registering extreme annoyance.

'So I'm constantly complaining, am I?'

Amanda hesitated as she tried to compose her answer.

She realised that she'd probably overstepped the mark. She might be Sister in Charge of Outpatients but she wasn't in charge of the highly skilled consultants. If Clive made a formal complaint about the way she handled the medical staff she would be for the high jump—and she couldn't afford to lose her job.

But during the first weeks of her appointment here she'd come to regard Clive as a close friend. They'd been out to the theatre together. She'd started talking to him in the way she would talk to someone she could trust.

'Look, Clive, I was very grateful to you for the way you took me under your wing when I was first appointed to my new job. It's only recently that you seem to find fault with my administration work. Now, I really do try to look at every situation and—'

'So I took you under my wing, did I? Is that how you saw it?' Clive's eyes flashed dangerously. 'Couldn't you see that the way I treated you had something to do with the way I felt about you? Couldn't you see I was falling in love with you?'

'Clive, I'm sorry…I had no idea.'

It had crossed her mind that Clive might not have been thinking of her as a platonic friend but she'd ignored it.

'You had no idea!' he repeated. 'That was because as soon as Edward arrived you were so besotted with him that—'

'I don't have to listen to this.' She stood up and turned away, but he grabbed her by the wrist.

'Tell me one thing, Amanda. Is this a permanent relationship? Or will lover boy move on when he gets bored? He's been married before, you know, and he left her at the other side of the world so that he could—'

'Edward has told me all about his marriage,' she broke in. 'And, whatever you've heard, remember there are two sides to every story.'

He let go her wrist and sank back into his chair.

'From your tone of voice I gather that you're going for a permanent relationship, then. The grapevine is buzzing with stories of how you're always together. They're betting on wedding bells but I'm not so sure.'

'I'm not so sure, either,' she said quietly as she moved towards the door.

He hurried after her and stood in front of it. 'Does that mean I'm in with a chance, then?'

She gave him a wry smile. All thoughts about her career prospects had vanished after Clive's emotional outburst. He might be a well-respected consultant, but he was only a little boy at heart. And a lonely little boy at that!

'Full marks for trying,' she said. 'But I'm a very independent woman. I don't need a man. If my relationship with Edward doesn't work out, I'll need a long period of independence to recover.'

Through the kitchen window, she could see the orange tints of the sunset vanishing behind the darkened buildings. It had been quite a day! First her sister's startling revelations and then Clive...

The phone was ringing. She dashed across the kitchen.

'Sorry I'm so late, Amanda. I couldn't call before because I was in the middle of a tricky abdominal operation.'

She could feel her heart giving a little hop, skip and a jump at the sound of Edward's voice, followed quickly by a lowering of her spirits as she wondered if he was calling to say he wasn't coming round.

'I cooked a chicken casserole.'

She was beginning to sound just like her mother! Except that she mustn't make him feel guilty if he was going to stand her up. She mustn't encroach on his precious freedom. But she wanted him so much, tonight...

'Great! I'm starving! Be with you in a few minutes.'

She was smiling as she replaced the receiver. No wonder the grapevine was humming when Edward dashed home to eat her chicken casserole! It typified domestic bliss. The little woman slaving away over a hot stove so that she could wait upon her beloved man when he came in, however late...

But the reality was quite different. They were both of them playing a role that was very fragile. And, in Edward's case, he was certainly getting the best of both worlds: he'd retained his independence but still had the dutiful little woman in attendance.

She decided to check on the casserole. It was looking decidedly dehydrated. Carefully, she mixed a chicken stock cube with water, rinsed a couple of mushrooms under the tap and stirred everything in. With the addition of half a green pepper and a small tomato it looked quite appetising again. She gave it another stir and popped it back in the oven.

When she heard Edward's car in the drive she tried to control her emotions. Slowly, she walked to the door and opened it, waiting with a welcoming smile as she always did. She planned to hold something back tonight, perhaps make him question her feelings for him, perhaps...

But the moment he took her in his arms she knew she was a slave to her emotions again! He pulled her against him, his lips tantalising her as they settled over hers. He led her inside, his arm round her waist, settling her head against his shoulder.

'Would you like a glass of wine before supper?' she asked quietly.

'Let's take the bottle with us and go to bed. I want to make love to you, Amanda. I've been longing for this moment all day.'

Tantalising, erotic, liquid sensations began to well up deep down inside her as he held her close. Supper could wait! Food wasn't important when they were both love-starved.

Their lovemaking was slow, unhurried, a dream-like experience between two people who had shared so many intimate, passionate moments that their bodies fused together so naturally, making them seem like one person.

Afterwards, as Amanda lay in the crook of Edward's arm, still conscious of the vibrant, climactic waves that had driven away all feeling of mundane reality, she found herself holding back the tears.

'Darling, what's the matter?' Edward was kissing her cheek as if trying to stem the flow.

'I think I'm crying because I'm so happy.'

'Well, I wouldn't like to see you cry if you were sad,' he said gently. 'Are you sure that...?'

She took a deep breath. 'I think it's because I feel it can't last—this idyllic state, I mean. When we make love, it's as if the real world doesn't exist. And then we have to come down from cloud nine.'

He pulled himself up to a sitting position, rearranging the pillows behind their heads and reaching for the wine bottle. He handed her a glass and she lay back with her head against his shoulder.

'Reality isn't so bad for either of us,' he said slowly.

'We've both got good jobs, good prospects, comfortable homes...'

'But how long can we go on like this?' There, she'd said it!

He was watching her with an enigmatic expression. 'But I thought you said you were happy, Amanda.'

'I am, but sometimes...'

She broke off, knowing that she'd said enough. Edward hadn't taken the bait, hadn't rushed in and said he understood how she felt and why didn't they get married and live happily ever after. That sort of thing only happened in fairy tales!

She pulled herself away and swung her legs over the side of the bed. 'I hope that casserole isn't ruined completely.'

In the kitchen, as she padded around barefoot in her dressing gown, she told herself she had to face facts. Edward was happy with the way things were and she would make the best of it...for as long as it lasted. She wasn't going to spoil their present exciting relationship with thoughts about the uncertain future.

But in the morning, as Edward dragged himself out of bed as soon as the alarm clock sounded, saying that he wanted to go back to his flat in the Barbican, she found herself wondering again how much longer she could continue the pretence.

CHAPTER NINE

AMANDA rustled her boots through the brown and yellow leaves on the woodland path at the bottom of the garden, revelling in the feel of the crisp October air. She'd walked down to the river by herself after breakfast to get away from the rest of the family. She needed to think.

Weddings were always disturbing occasions, and this one in particular was definitely making her reassess where she was going in her life. It was a month since she'd met Yvonne in the park and offered her support. During the intervening weeks, Yvonne had telephoned her more times than she'd ever done in the whole of her life before. And for the first time in their lives the sisters had become close—just as sisters were supposed to be.

She raised her eyes as she heard the sound of a car coming over the brow of the hill. Yes, it was Edward. She glanced at her watch. He'd made good time from London. He must have left the city very early. She felt a surge of loving emotion as she watched the steel-grey car coming up the drive. Although there was a keen wind, Edward was driving with the top down. He looked very dashing and debonair with his dark hair encased in a grey hat, and a woollen scarf casually entwined around his neck.

She broke into a run, unable to contain her excitement. They'd been apart for three whole days while she'd been helping her sister with the wedding preparations. She'd taken a holiday from hospital and it had seemed like a month without Edward. She'd also missed Tom and wished she could have persuaded him to come with her.

She'd pointed out that she could get permission for him

to miss three days' school. He was well ahead in his class—somewhere near the top, his teacher had told her—so he'd easily have been able to catch up when he'd got back. But Tom was adamant that he didn't want to miss football and swimming for a boring old wedding. And he didn't want to have to keep clean and tidy for his granny either!

She'd understood how he felt. She'd been in his position many times herself! And something about the set of his young jaw told her that he'd inherited her streak of obstinacy. There was no way she'd be able to talk this young man into anything he didn't want to do in the future—not that she wanted to! From her own experience she was convinced that people should be allowed to make up their own minds.

Mark had been thrilled that Tom was coming to stay for a few days. Alice hadn't started work at the supermarket yet. The early morning shift was full so she was waiting for a vacancy on the mid-morning to mid-afternoon shift especially designed for mothers with children. So Amanda had no worries about Tom apart from the fact that she wished he'd been with her in this house that used to be her home but where she now felt like a stranger.

Edward was swinging his legs over the side of the car and running towards her. She felt as if she were in a slow-motion film as she hurried to meet him halfway. He pulled her against him. She lifted her face for his kiss and as their lips joined she gave an involuntary sigh of contentment.

From the depths of her renewed happiness, she became suddenly aware that her mother was standing in the open doorway, and she didn't want to make the full extent of their relationship blatantly obvious. Her mother had already queried Edward's name on the guest list but Yvonne had insisted she wanted him to be at her wedding.

Amanda moved apart from Edward, but realised that she wanted desperately to be alone with him if only for a few minutes before they were claimed by the events of the day.

'I'll help Edward take his luggage to his old room, Mum,' she called, picking up his camera case and draping the garment bag that held his suit over her arm.

'I've asked Mrs Brown to prepare the guest room for Edward,' Felicity Grayson said quietly. 'I thought he would prefer that to his room over the stables. It can become quite chilly in there at this time of the year.'

Amanda could see the worry lines etched on her mother's face as she spoke. In the past month she'd had her life turned upside down by the one daughter she'd thought she could trust to uphold the family traditions. But it seemed as if it had brought her up to date and she was, at last, beginning to accept the fact that both her daughters had finally grown up.

Edward held out his hand to shake with Felicity. 'Thank you, Dr Grayson.'

He might be on first name terms with Amanda's father, but her mother still held herself aloof. He picked up his brown leather weekend case and followed Amanda into the house. Stepping inside the guest room, Amanda turned and saw that Edward was trying not to laugh.

'So I'm accepted at last, am I?' he said quietly.

He was glancing around at the highly polished oak floor partly covered by Persian rugs. The long, sashed windows were draped with ruby-red velvet curtains which added to the splendour of the Queen Anne dressing table, chairs, wardrobe and four-poster bed.

'To what do I owe this honour?'

Amanda sank down onto the white counterpane and put out her hand towards Edward. 'I really couldn't imagine.

Maybe it's Mummy's way of saying you're accepted. Come and sit beside me and I'll tell you all the news.'

He leaned down and kissed her, but remained standing. 'If I sit down beside you on that sexy-looking cover I won't be able to control myself. I'll want to pull you between the sheets and…'

She squealed as he put both hands on her shoulders. 'Edward! There isn't time!'

She was giving him a mock reprimand but she could feel the rise in her spirits that she'd lacked over the past three days. She was beginning to realise that life without Edward seemed like only half a life and that was a scary thought. She'd never depended on anybody in her life. How would she cope if she had to live without him again?

Edward took hold of her hand and led her over to the window-seat. 'You'll be safer here,' he said with a rakish grin. 'I expect your gardener is lurking in the rose garden with instructions to shoot if I so much as lay a finger on you. So how come I qualify for the guest room?'

Amanda smiled. 'My mother's been in a state of shock since Yvonne told her she was pregnant and was going to marry Trevor.'

He put an arm loosely across the back of the window-seat. 'I can imagine. Not exactly the sort of behaviour she would expect from her favourite daughter. But how on earth did Yvonne persuade Trevor they should get married? I remember she told us she was petrified because he had a grown-up family and she didn't think he would want to start another one.'

'It was the other way round,' Amanda said quickly. 'Why is it always assumed that it's the woman who's hell-bent on marriage and the poor man falls in with their wishes?'

He raised an eyebrow and in a deadpan voice said, 'Well, isn't it?'

She picked up one of the cretonne cushions and aimed it at his head. He ducked and pulled her into his arms. She relaxed against him and tried not to think about how much she wished it were their wedding that was taking place today.

'Not at all,' she said huffily. 'Lots of women don't see the need for marriage nowadays. I don't expect Yvonne would have considered getting married if she hadn't been pregnant. When children are involved it changes everything. Yvonne told me that Trevor was over the moon when she told him they were expecting a baby. But he insisted they get married as soon as possible.'

'How romantic!'

Amanda smiled. 'Yvonne told me he's terribly conventional and wanted to make an honest woman of her before tongues start wagging.'

'What time's the wedding?'

'Twelve noon, so we'd better get a move on. I'll go and change and meet you downstairs.'

Edward's eyes, as Amanda walked into the sitting room in her long, cream silk dress, registered tenderness and admiration. She wanted to rush into his arms but she restrained the feeling as she looked around at the assembled company.

Her mother and father were standing one on either side of the fireplace where a log fire, liberally scattered with pine cones, sent a sweet-smelling aroma wafting around the room. Yvonne was sitting on the sofa, her long white dress spread out over the cushions. Edward was standing by the window, looking terribly handsome in a slim-fitting grey morning suit that showed off his tall, athletic figure to perfection.

He crossed the room and stood beside her. 'You look lovely, Amanda.'

'Thank you,' she replied in what she decided was a demure tone quite unlike her usual voice. Standing beside Edward, dressed as they both were, she felt as if she were in a scene from *Pride and Prejudice*!

She accepted a small glass of sherry from her father, who was looking unusually smart and rather self-conscious in his pinstripe trousers and black jacket.

Her father raised his glass. 'To the bride!'

Yvonne smiled and raised hers. 'Thanks, Dad.' She looked around the room. 'You've all been great to me…you really have. It's all been such a change in my life. I'd never planned to start a family before…'

Felicity cleared her throat. 'Quite, dear. Life is what happens to you when you're making your elaborate plans. I hope you'll be very happy in your chosen…with your chosen husband. Trevor seems a very likeable sort of man.'

'Very dependable,' Geoffrey said, nodding in agreement with his wife. 'He's getting on a bit now, but I've known him since he was a young man, of course, and—'

'Dad, he's only fifty-five,' Yvonne said, indignantly trying to pull herself off the sofa and failing miserably due to a combination of the facts that she wasn't used to the swollen feeling of her four-month pregnancy and she was totally unpractised at wearing the long gown created specially for her in the designer boutique in Leeds.

'I can't think why I let Trevor talk me into a white wedding,' she said, flopping back against the cushions. 'Everybody will be staring at the bump under my flowers and whispering that—'

'Let them whisper if it makes them happy,' Amanda said, quickly walking over to her sister's side and sinking down on the floor at her feet.

'There's little enough tittle-tattle in this neck of the woods to keep them going through the winter. They'll be thrilled to know that Trevor's going to be a father again. The postman told me he's a very popular character in the village. He farms the largest area in this part of Yorkshire, so he's what the locals call a good catch!'

She was smiling at her sister, hoping that she could see the joke as she effected a Yorkshire accent. 'Come on, admit it, you've always wanted to be a farmer's wife, haven't you?'

Yvonne giggled. 'I can't think of anything I'd like better than milking the cows before I go into surgery in the morning.'

'Oh, Trevor has a lot of farm hands to do the rough work,' Felicity put in quickly, completely unaware that her daughters were having a joke with each other.

Edward grasped Yvonne's hands, pulling her to her feet. 'If it's any consolation, Dr Soon-to-be-farmer's-wife, you still look extremely slim. And everybody's going to find out about the baby soon enough. You can't push the pram around under a maternity smock, can you?'

Yvonne was giggling again. Her mother picked up the sherry decanter and removed it to the far end of the room.

'No more sherry for Yvonne, dear,' Felicity whispered to Geoffrey as she passed him. 'She's had two already and it's not good for the baby.'

Walking down the aisle behind her sister, Amanda found herself feeling highly sentimental and positively nostalgic. Glancing around carefully as she tried not to trip over Yvonne's long dress, she could see that the church was packed. And everyone was smiling, admiringly, at the bridal procession.

She smiled back, not sure about the protocol on these occasions and finding it difficult not to wave her freesia and lily of the valley bouquet at a couple of old school friends she could see in the back pew. She'd only been a bridesmaid twice before and then, as a very small child, she'd been pushed and prodded into good behaviour by tall, regal ladies with strange-smelling perfumes whose long, swirling skirts had tickled her nose as she'd waited in the porch.

She realised that this was her third time as a bridesmaid. Wasn't there some superstitious saying that if you were three times a bridesmaid you would never be a bride?

They were nearing the altar now. She caught a glimpse of Edward, squashed in between two large ladies who might or might not have been her mother's sisters. It was so long since she'd met any of her family. But she would no doubt find out at the reception.

The actual ceremony passed off without a hitch. Amanda felt relieved at the confident way the bridegroom declared his vows. From what she'd seen of him so far, her new brother-in-law would make her sister happy.

Going back down the aisle, she was paired off with one of Trevor's tall, strapping sons, florid of complexion from his outdoor life on the farm. She found herself wondering if he was looking forward to having a baby brother or sister around the farm.

Yvonne had told her she was planning to drive in to the Grayson practice from the farm each morning and have out-of-hours calls put to her there. The arrangement hadn't pleased either of her parents. Her mother was now planning to come back from her retirement until all the problems caused by this momentous change in the family life plan had been ironed out.

As she walked out into the pale autumnal sunshine Amanda sensed that Yvonne's wedding and pregnancy were causing an even bigger disruption to the harmony of the Grayson practice than she'd created herself twelve years ago.

Edward, she could see, was escorting the two large

ladies to one of the waiting ribbon-festooned cars. He turned as he helped them inside and gave her a discreet wave. She had an intense longing to rush across and escape with him but she knew she would have to hold her feelings in check—at least until after the reception.

By the time they'd reached the end of the wedding reception the whole of the village knew that there was a baby on the way. Yvonne, fortified by a couple of glasses of champagne, had suddenly found herself proud to be announcing the news and accepting the congratulations.

The family relations and guests from the village had gathered in the marquee that had been erected on the side lawn, connected by a covered walkway to the kitchen. As Amanda passed among them she heard a few unsavoury snippets that she chose not to pass on to her sister.

'A good thing Trevor changed his doctor before all this started…'

'I never thought I'd see the day when Miss Prim and Proper would…'

'Dr Felicity doesn't look too happy today. You'd think the mother of the bride…'

Amanda kept on walking until she was outside the marquee. The evening sun was slanting across the valley, casting golden shadows. She picked up an acorn from under the tall oak tree by the kitchen window and hurled it as far as she could into the shrubbery just as she had done as a child.

'Was that frustration?'

She turned at the welcome sound of Edward's voice. 'Probably. I just feel the need to escape.'

He gave her a rakish grin. 'Me too. But you won't get very far in that dress.'

She laughed. 'I can hitch up my skirts!' She pulled at the restricting silk and stuffed the hems of her skirt and petticoat underneath the cream suede belt that encircled her waist.

'Don't look!' she exhorted Edward as she removed her white court shoes and peeled off her tights.

There was something terribly wicked about removing her tights in front of him. She knew that on the occasions when they were both fired up with intense desire for each other and couldn't wait to put skin against skin, she never even noticed who was unbuttoning what. But out here in the cooling atmosphere of the late afternoon, only yards from the wedding marquee, she felt she had to preserve a modicum of decency. Even if she was standing with her skirts rolled up above her knees!

'Come on, Edward!' She grabbed his hand.

'Can I open my eyes now?'

She laughed as he pretended to open one eye and then the other, before his face creased into a rakish grin.

'I hope you've got thick skin on the soles of your feet.'

'I've got thick skin everywhere. Just try and catch me,' she declared as she began to race over the grass.

The wet grass soothed her feet, the cool, fresh air filled her lungs and she felt alive again. As Edward's hands grabbed her by the waist she stopped and allowed him to pull her against him. They were out of sight of the house, standing under the oak tree where there had been a swing suspended from one of the branches when she'd been a child, she remembered.

She savoured the taste of his lips as she pressed herself against him beneath the old tree.

'Will you come to my room tonight?' Edward asked huskily.

She drew in her breath. 'I can't, Edward. I really can't. I know it sounds peculiar for a woman of thirty to admit, but when I'm in my parents' home I have to abide by their rules. That's why I had to leave home all those years ago. They were stifling the life out of me. They don't mean to do it; they can't help the way they're made any more than I can.'

'Well, if I'm going to have to spend the night in that palatial ivory tower all by myself I think I'll go back to London,' he said, in a sorrowful tone.

'No, oh, Edward, you wouldn't leave me...' She broke off, embarrassed at disclosing how much she'd come to depend on him.

He pulled her closer. 'Only joking. Of course I wouldn't go off and leave you, knowing how you hate the long journey by bus and train. So why don't we both escape together? The bride and groom are off to catch their plane from the airport soon; the guests are beginning to go home. I would imagine your parents would enjoy a bit of peace and quiet this evening.'

It was an intriguing idea and, the more she thought about it, the more she agreed that it would solve a lot of problems.

She gave a sigh of relief. 'Let's go back to the house and change. We can be home in four hours.'

He raised an eyebrow. 'Home? My place or yours?'

She laughed. 'Does it matter?'

CHAPTER TEN

THE busy London street was shrouded in thick November fog as Amanda hurried towards the hospital. Edward's telephone call had awakened her in the early hours, since when she'd had to make arrangements with Alice about looking after Tom and prepare a list of the changes she would have to make to her daily routine in Outpatients.

The shopping mall was still closed as she hurried in through the main door and went along to her room. Sitting down at her desk, she switched on her computer and prepared to relay messages through to various colleagues alerting them to the fact that she would be in the operating theatre during the morning.

For the past few weeks, ever since it had been discovered that their little patient, William Fairburn, had malignant tumours in both kidneys, the hospital had been on the list for a transplant donor for him. She tried to tell herself that she shouldn't have favourites but this precious little lamb had always tugged at her heartstrings.

Staring at the computer screen now, she remembered the first time that William had arrived in Outpatients. She could see his dear little face quite vividly as he bravely tried to hold back the tears caused by his awful tummy ache.

It had been the day of the school coach crash, she remembered. Accident and Emergency had been snowed under with the victims and had sent William along to Outpatients. If it had been any other day she would never have met the brave little boy. And she wouldn't have become so emotionally involved in the outcome of his treatment.

Her phone was ringing. 'Sister Grayson here...oh, it's you, Edward. I'm just—'

'If you want to join the team you'll have to come now, Amanda. The donor team have switched off the ventilator and we're preparing the recipient for surgery now.'

Edward sounded so professional—and a bit stressed. Understandable when there was so much at stake. 'I'm on my way.'

As she waited for the lift that would take her up to the operating theatres she felt a frisson of apprehension. It was several years since she'd worked in theatre, so Edward wouldn't have assigned her to do anything difficult. Because the operation was taking place at such short notice, there had been an overnight call-out of theatre staff who weren't already scheduled for routine operations this morning.

Edward had been asked to head the team which was responsible for putting the donor kidneys into William. As soon as she'd taken his call this morning she'd agreed to assist in any way he thought appropriate.

Going up now in the lift, she felt relieved that she wasn't on the team who had to remove the kidneys from the child who'd died. The only consolation the poor parents of this child would have was that they were helping another child to live, because without new kidneys William wouldn't survive more than a few weeks. The last time she'd seen him, in the dialysis unit, he'd been very weak and had barely recognised her.

She walked out of the lift, taking a deep breath to steady her nerves before pushing open the swing doors of Theatre One. Edward was crossing from the scrub room to the main operating room. He changed directions and came towards her. She felt a surge of gratitude that he hadn't ignored her, because he was plainly under considerable stress and due to her lowly position in the theatre pecking order he could have been excused for getting on with his important work.

'Are you OK, Amanda? You're sure you—?'

'I want to be part of the team,' she said quickly. 'I know I shouldn't be so emotionally involved with William but I can't help thinking how I would feel if this was Tom waiting for a life-saving operation.'

He raised one eyebrow above his mask. 'Try to be objective, Amanda, otherwise—'

'I know, I know.' She drew in her breath. 'I am objective.'

Out of the corner of her eye she could see Theatre Sister approaching. She tried to look totally professional as she smiled up at Edward.

'Thank you for your advice, Mr Burrows!'

Edward moved away as Theatre Sister took over.

'Ah, Sister Grayson, how good of you to join us. If you'd like to come this way and start to scrub up, I'll get one of my nurses to fix you up with a sterile gown. You won't mind staying at the side of the theatre, will you? You'll be a great help with the fetching and carrying from that position—swabs and utensils and so on. I'll explain when we get into theatre…'

Amanda told Theatre Sister that she didn't mind what she did so long as she felt she was helping in some way.

The bright lights over the table were dazzling as she went into the theatre, suitably gowned and masked. Strange to think that the tiny, shrunken, motionless form on the table was the lively little boy she'd treated in Outpatients.

From her vantage point near the door she could see Edward poised over the patient.

'Scalpel, Sister.'

She held her breath as she watched him making the first incision, before beginning to cut through the layers of tissue beneath the skin. He raised his eyes briefly as a member of the donor team came in with a container which held the two precious kidneys.

Theatre Sister signalled to one of her nurses to place the container near to the table. Edward continued with the operation. Amanda thought he was looking remarkably cool and collected. One of the team around the table passed her a kidney dish of swabs and pieces of tissue. She placed it at the side of the room in the specified section where everything would be checked before incineration or pathological testing at the end of the operation.

She saw with relief that Edward was now removing the two diseased kidneys. These would be taken away to help with research into the causes of malignant tumours.

Replacing the diseased kidneys with the healthy kidneys seemed a more simple operation than she remembered from her nursing training. Things had moved on since then. Techniques and equipment had improved considerably. And surgeons were more skilled, she thought, watching the deft movements of Edward's fingers as he plumbed in the new organs.

'There, the kidneys are working.' He was standing back, smiling with relief at the successful outcome of the operation. 'With the skilful post-operative care for which St Elizabeth's is renowned, young William should pull through nicely.'

Amanda knew this was the signal for the team to begin the clearing up process. She was about to begin when she realised that Edward was standing right beside her.

'Would you like to special William until he's round from the anaesthetic, Sister Grayson?'

Would she! 'Of course, Mr Burrows.'

*   *   *

'I'm glad you asked me to special William until he came round,' Amanda said, leaning forward across her desk to pour more coffee into Edward's cup. 'I'd felt pretty useless until then.'

'"They also serve who only stand and wait,"' he said wryly. 'I'm going along to see William at the end of the afternoon, otherwise it's up to the surgical consultant and his team to take care of him.'

'He was a good colour when I left him. Temperature normal, no sign of infection...'

'You shouldn't get infection if the surgeon has done his job properly.'

She hesitated. 'You obviously enjoy surgery, and you're pretty good at it...'

He leaned forward. 'Only pretty good?'

'OK, then, you're exceptionally skilled.'

'Don't go over the top. Why all the sudden compliments?'

'I'm simply stating a fact.' She hesitated. 'So I've often wondered why you'd taken this job in Outpatients?'

His eyes flickered. 'Because I'd heard all about the beauty of the sister in charge and—'

'Come on, be serious, Edward. What made you change from being a full-time surgeon?'

She heard the swift intake of his breath before he began to speak again in a low, gravelly voice. 'I had a bad experience. Soon after I'd got my fellowship exams I was appointed to a consultancy in a regional hospital in Wales. I was the first person to perform transplant surgery there. I thought I had a good team...'

She came round the side of the desk and leaned against it, close enough to watch the changing expressions on his face. He was suffering in some way. She felt a sense of apprehension as she leaned forward and put her hand on his shoulder. He barely seemed to notice her gesture as he gazed in front of him.

'You thought you had a good team?' she repeated. 'But what was the reality?'

'There was one member of my team I was doubtful about from the start. He had been an alcoholic but had been cured for over five years. I inherited him as my registrar from the previous consultant who told me he was an excellent surgeon but that I should keep a watchful eye in case he relapsed.

'During my first year as a consultant there, he behaved impeccably. He was very talented and of immense value to the surgical team. At first I constantly checked his work and his social life to make sure that the patients were one hundred per cent safe in his hands. Little by little I began to relax with him; I told myself that he was completely cured. And I stopped checking up on him.'

She saw the anguished expression in his eyes as she knelt down beside him, taking his hands in her own. 'What happened?'

'I put…I won't tell you his name because it was in all the papers…I put my registrar in charge of removing a malignant tumour…and the patient died on the table. If I'd only checked up I would have found that his wife had left him and he'd spent the night drinking. He was in no fit state to perform…'

'But I remember the case,' Amanda said quickly. 'The court decided that the patient's chance of living beyond a few months was very slim. I remember the doctor was reprimanded and—'

'But a patient died on the table! It doesn't matter whether he had a few months or a few years to live! I was the consultant in charge of his case and I should have checked that my staff were fit to perform the operation. I decided there and then that I couldn't stand the responsibility of being in charge of life-and-death situations.'

She released his hand. 'I think you're being very hard on yourself.'

'Maybe I am,' he said slowly. 'But that's the way I'm made. I gave in my notice immediately after the court case.'

'But you weren't even mentioned in the paper—not the one I read,' she added quickly. 'I would have remembered your name because…well, you had a profound effect on me when you were working for my father and…'

He didn't seem to have picked up on the fact that she'd always carried a torch for him, that he'd been constantly in her thoughts over the years in between.

'I wasn't asked to give evidence,' he said quietly. 'My registrar was deemed to have bungled the operation and was struck off. Shortly afterwards he went into a clinic for another cure. That was when I decided to hang up my scalpel.'

He gave her a wry smile. 'That's a mixed metaphor if ever I made one, isn't it? But you know what I mean.'

'So you gave up surgery because somebody else made a mistake?'

'As I've told you, he was my junior. I was in charge of him. I gave in my notice and took a post in Outpatients in a hospital in Scotland.'

'You've certainly travelled around a bit!'

He smiled. 'You know what they say about a rolling stone.' He hesitated. 'Which is why I've decided it's time to move on again—before I start gathering moss.'

She felt a cold hand clutching at her heart. 'What do you mean, Edward?'

'This morning was the first time I felt totally confident again in the operating theatre. I had no premonitions of disaster when I started and I was pleased with the way all the staff accomplished their tasks—you included, Amanda.'

'Don't overdo the compliments!' she said, her tone more acerbic than she'd intended. 'I was simply doing my job.' The worry that Edward might be moving on was making her tetchy. 'So you're not happy with the outpatient department at St Elizabeth's?'

He hesitated before lifting his eyes to hers. 'I'm extremely happy with the whole set-up. But I need to move on, to go back into full-time surgery and—'

'So, when do you plan to leave Outpatients?' she asked, surprised at how calm her voice sounded as she tried desperately to calm her turbulent emotions.

'At the end of April. When my contract with Outpatients expires, I won't renew it. I know it won't be easy to find the sort of surgical job I want but I'll just have to keep searching. It's something I have to do. You do understand, don't you, Amanda?'

She swivelled her chair round so that she was facing the computer screen, away from Edward.

Her professional persona was taking over; her emotions were on hold, packed neatly into an icebox stored deep down inside her. She felt exactly as she had done when she'd first been abandoned, with the prospect of bringing a child into an unknown future by herself. She'd survived on her own then and she would survive now. She had her interesting and satisfying work, and the most wonderful son in the world. She was financially secure. She had everything she needed.

'Of course I understand, Edward. It's good to know you've finally found your true career,' she said, with a determined effort at control. 'Surgery must be much more satisfying than administration.'

He stood up, moving round to put his hands on her shoulders. She tensed, trying desperately not to feel moved at the touch of his fingers. She was a professional. Edward was a colleague, soon to be leaving the department, going on somewhere without her.

'I knew you'd understand,' he said in a relieved tone. 'So, what are your plans for this evening?'

'Alice and I are taking the boys to the cinema,' she said, surprising herself at the ease with which she could invent a little white lie.

He pressed his lips, briefly, against her cheek. 'See you tomorrow, then.'

She didn't move. It was as if she'd been turned to stone. But as she heard him close the door she buried her head in her hands and sobbed. Edward was a rolling stone and she couldn't change him. She was glad she hadn't tried! She would survive. She always had done before when the going had got tough.

She went into her little cloakroom and splashed cold water over her face before attempting to smile at herself in the mirror. That was better! The idea of taking the boys to the cinema began to take hold. This was just the sort of off-duty activity she had to cultivate from now on. She had to let herself down gently from the heights of ecstasy she'd reached with Edward so that, when he actually left her, she wouldn't feel the pain of separation so acutely.

CHAPTER ELEVEN

THROUGHOUT the dark days of December and January, Amanda kept her emotions firmly in check. She made a point of being unavailable as often as she could when Edward asked her out. Twice, she agreed to go to the theatre, and one evening they went to a restaurant, but she forced herself to accept that these brief encounters were merely temporary.

She made excuses about being tired at the end of the evening so that she didn't have to be alone with Edward. She didn't want to reopen the emotional wounds that she hoped were beginning to heal. Little by little, she sensed that Edward, too, was drawing apart from her. Their affair was lapsing into a platonic friendship. She told herself that this was what she wanted. This was the only way she was going to survive.

At Christmas, she took Tom home to her parents' for a few days, throwing herself into the festivities with as much physical energy as she could muster. Inside, she felt numb, but she went through all the motions which the festive season required, ensuring that Tom and her parents enjoyed themselves. The only bright spot in the gloom of January was the wedding of Nikki Barclay to her handsome Australian. Although she wasn't invited to the wedding, Amanda heard plenty from the people who did go, particularly the little flowergirls, who were so excited they collared everyone in Outpatients to tell them all about the wonderful day.

As the weeks went by, she convinced herself that she was over the first hurdle. Edward's physical presence in

Outpatients still affected her more than she cared to think about, but she told herself that she would recover as soon as he found his surgical niche and left the hospital.

Occasionally she allowed herself the luxury of hoping that there would be a vacant surgical post at Lizzie's but, knowing how ambitious he was, she discounted that idea. All the top surgical jobs were taken and Edward wouldn't want to take a step down the career ladder. No, he was going to spread his wings and fly away and she was going to get on with the business of rebuilding her life.

On a cold, February morning, with flurries of soft snow sticking to the windows in Orthopaedic Outpatients, she found, as she always did, that immersing herself totally in her work took away the heartache that plagued her whenever she had time to think about the future.

Very carefully, she helped young David to climb off the examination couch. The new prosthesis hadn't been as comfortable as the old one. She'd helped Clive to fit a completely different, state-of-the-art, very expensive new kind and they were hoping that this would prove successful.

She walked over to the door with her young patient and his mother.

'I hope you realise you're one of the few patients in England to be given one of these brilliant new superlegs, young man,' Clive said.

David swivelled round, a broad grin on his face. 'You told me the last one was a superleg but I didn't like it. I'll give you my report on this one next time and you can quote me in one of those articles in the medical magazines.'

His mother ruffled his hair, fondly. 'Don't be so cheeky, David.' She looked at the consultant. 'He's forever got his head in a science book, Doctor. Says he's going to be a doctor.'

Amanda smiled. 'I think you'd make a very good doctor, David.'

'Do you?' The little boy looked up at her. 'Can I work in this hospital?'

'You wait until you're trained, David, and then we'll consider you.'

Amanda went into the consulting room and began to change the sheet. She was aware that Clive had followed her in and was leaning against the trolley.

'So, lover boy is leaving Outpatients, is he?'

She straightened up and faced him across the couch. 'Excuse me?'

'Oh, haven't you heard? Hasn't he told you? Edward's job is advertised in the latest edition of—'

'I knew there was a possibility he wouldn't renew his contract at the end of April,' she said carefully, annoyed that she hadn't been informed about this latest development. 'I expect Edward also told me the post was going to be advertised soon. Yes, I expect it slipped my mind.'

As she quickly bent her head to continue her task, she knew she was a rotten liar.

'Pull the other one, Amanda! You wouldn't have forgotten anything so important to you. He's sneaking off, isn't he? And you of all people haven't heard about it. I know what I'd do if he were my partner...'

'Edward is not my partner. He—'

She broke off, aware that the door had opened, that Edward had come in and was standing right behind Clive.

Clive turned round and frowned. 'You may still be in charge of Outpatients, Mr Burrows, but this is my consulting room and I'll thank you to knock before you come in and break up a private conversation.'

Edward's face was white with anger. 'I did knock but you were making so much noise you didn't hear. And as the conversation is all about me I think I've got a right to hear it.'

Clive gave a triumphant smile. 'I was just informing Amanda that your job is advertised in the medical press, and I was astounded to hear you hadn't had the decency to inform our sister in charge.'

'You're referring to the advertisement that came out today, I presume. I didn't want to bother Amanda with such a trivial task as advertising for staff so I took it upon myself.'

Edward looked directly across at Amanda. 'If you could spare a few minutes of your valuable time in my consulting room…within the next hour or so…?'

He turned on his heel and left the room.

Amanda drew in her breath to steady her nerves. It was a whole week since she'd seen Edward. She'd deliberately ignored his messages on her answering machine on three separate occasions.

Her fingers moved automatically as she tucked in the sheet across the couch.

'You'd better go and see what Edward wants,' Clive said evenly. 'He probably wants to bid you a fond farewell.'

'You're right,' she said absently. 'I'll call Sister in from your registrar's clinic.'

'I'll call her myself,' he said, moving over to the desk. 'I didn't tell you that our new sister is turning out better than I thought.'

She turned at the door. 'So her work is improving, is it?'

He grinned. 'Let's say her work is adequate but she has other compensations. In fact I've taken quite a shine to her—in my off duty, that is. Edward's choice from the agency was very sound. He knows how to pick them.'

'I'm glad you're…suited. Now, if you'll excuse me.'

*   *   *

Edward had left the door to his consulting room open. She stepped gingerly over the threshold. He was on the phone and waved an arm for her to sit down. For a few seconds, she felt like a naughty schoolgirl who'd been summoned to the headmaster's study.

He put the phone down and faced her, his face devoid of any expression.

'I called you in to explain why you hadn't been informed about my advertisement.'

She averted her eyes and stared out of the window, noticing that the snow was already melting as a pale, wintry sun attempted to shine over the white roofs. Soon it would be spring, with picnics in the park and dutiful visits to her parents when she would escape over the moors and remember that day when she and Edward had seemed so close. Got to be brave...don't let him see you're suffering.

'It doesn't matter. I would have heard through the usual channels in due course, I expect. If that's the only reason you called me in...'

'It's not!' He stood up and moved round the desk. 'I need to know that you approve of the move I'm making.'

She stared up at him and saw that a nerve in his cheek was quivering. He looked more nervous than she'd ever seen him.

'Why should you need my approval?' she asked quietly. 'You've always done exactly as you pleased without consulting me. Why now, when you're just about to leave the hospital, should it make any difference what I think?'

'I'm not leaving the hospital,' he said. 'The hospital board has created a specialist surgical post for me, which I'll take up at the beginning of May. I'll be in charge of coordinating the surgical teams required for transplant operations to ensure minimum disruption in the routine surgery.'

'But why didn't you tell me before?' She wanted to

dance for joy! 'I thought…and when Clive said you'd already advertised…'

'I didn't advertise. The hospital board advertised my post last week when they confirmed my new surgical appointment. I'd been considering applying for a couple of posts in London when the board informed me they didn't want to lose me. Anyway, it was never my intention to move away from this area. I wanted to stay within striking distance. I'd drawn a ring around the area I planned to work in when the hospital board came up with their brilliant idea. Initially, I was sworn to secrecy so I couldn't tell you about it whilst it was still under wraps, and you've been so distant and unapproachable during the last few weeks that—'

'I thought you were going to escape miles away from here, making sure you didn't have to commit yourself to a situation that was becoming too intense. I thought you were planning to be footloose and fancy free at the ripe old age of—'

'Hang about, what are you implying?' Edward's dark eyes flashed dangerously. 'Didn't we agree that we both enjoyed our freedom, that neither of us wanted to change anything in our lives? Why do you think I left before breakfast, before Tom came down from Alice's?'

She was utterly confused. 'Why did you?'

'Because if Tom knew I'd slept with you, I would have had to ask you to marry me and—'

'Not necessarily. He's very advanced for his age. He knows we're having an affair and he understands the implications.'

He pulled a wry face. 'I wish you'd told me. You've no idea how I hated leaving you behind and trekking across London.'

She smiled. 'To open the post that hadn't arrived?'

He laughed and she revelled once more in the relaxing sound she loved so much.

'I was only thinking of you. I knew how you didn't want to change the way you were living, how you valued your independence.'

'I used to think it was the most valuable part of my life,' she said quietly, almost to herself. 'Being able to close the door on the rest of the world and be mistress of my own little domain, with my wonderful son, my ever faithful cat and nobody to demand anything from me, but since…'

Her voice trailed away as she searched for the right words to tell him that ever since he'd come into her life her world had been turned upside down.

'Does that mean that if someone asked you to marry him there might be a chance you'd be willing to change your ideas?' he asked huskily.

She looked up into his expressive eyes. Was he getting a cold or was that moisture something to do with the tear ducts? Men didn't cry, did they? She had a lot to learn about the man in her life, but there would be a whole lifetime to learn it.

'Not just someone,' she said quietly. 'It would have to be a very special person. Someone tolerant, amusing, fun to be with; a man who likes children, has a good sense of humour…'

He gave her a rakish grin as he pulled her to her feet, cradling her head against his chest. 'You could put an advertisement in the lonely hearts column,' he whispered. 'If I applied, would I stand a chance?'

She raised her head and pulled his lips down towards hers. 'I'd give your application due consideration, Doctor.'

When he finally released her from their long, lingering

kiss he remained looking down at her with an expression of infinite tenderness.

Amanda ran a hand through her ruffled hair. 'Let's go and tell Tom the good news. I'd like him to be the first to know.'

Tom was as excited as Amanda had ever seen him when they explained that they were going to get married.

Edward had delayed the news until they were all sitting round the kitchen table, clutching a glass. Tom's glass contained cola, Edward's and Amanda's were brimming over with champagne.

Tom drained his glass in one fell swoop. 'Wow, that's fantastic. So will you be my dad?'

Edward hesitated and looked across at Amanda.

'Stepdad,' she said quietly. 'Do you know what—?'

'Yeah! My mate at school has one. Says he's great—took him to Disneyland.' He looked enquiringly at Edward. 'Have you ever been there?'

Edward smiled. 'Not yet, but I think it could be arranged.'

'Fantastic! But I can still call you Edward, can't I? And you'll still play football with me, won't you? I mean, you're not going to get all old and bad-tempered like some dads I've met?'

Edward smiled. 'Nothing will change, Tom; except we'll probably buy a house so that we've got more room and—'

Tom picked up Fluffy, who'd been circling the legs under the table demanding attention. 'And Fluffy can come as well, can't she?'

'Of course. Fluffy can be chief mouse-catcher. We'll look for a house with a garden so we can dispense with the cat tray and—'

'Can I go up and tell Mark and Alice?' Tom was already at the door.

Amanda laughed. 'Of course!'

The door slammed and she sipped her champagne, feeling a warm rosy glow creeping over her that had nothing to do with the alcohol content of her glass. Edward moved his chair closer and put his arm round her, pulling her head against his shoulder.

The phone rang. She reached for the portable in the middle of the table.

'Congratulations, Amanda!'

'Thanks, Alice.'

'Mark's asked if Tom can help him with his homework and stay the night.' Alice was giggling. 'Can you spare him?'

'On this occasion I think we probably can. Thanks again, Alice.'

Edward was standing up. 'What was all that about?'

'Alice has asked if Tom can stay the night.'

He scooped her up into his arms. 'So we have a whole night to ourselves.'

'And a lot of wedding plans to make,' Amanda said, clasping her arms around his neck.

'Let's plan the honeymoon first,' he said huskily as he carried her over to the bedroom.

EPILOGUE

THE fierce March winds that had gusted down the dale during the final days of preparation at the farm relented on the actual wedding day. Sitting beside her father in the white vintage wedding car, Amanda could see that the newborn lambs, playing in the fields that sloped down to the narrow lane, were enjoying the welcome warmth of the early spring sunshine.

The church was packed, just as it had been for her sister's wedding, but the way she felt as she walked down the aisle was completely different from the last time. She could smell the spring flowers that her mother and sister had arranged in every corner of the church, and this time she didn't have to be careful not to tread on the dress in front because she was leading the way.

And the bridegroom waiting at the altar was the most wonderful man in the world! Edward turned to look at her as she reached his side and, even through the veil that surrounded her, she could see the intensity of his love shining out of those dark, expressive eyes. To please the family, she'd gone along with convention and not allowed him to see her this morning; not even the tiniest peep! And she'd missed him so much as she'd put on her white silk and lace wedding dress.

Tonight she would make up for being without him for—how many hours was it now? She'd better concentrate...the vicar was beginning the questions they'd rehearsed. Was it really necessary to ask if she wanted to marry Edward John Burrows? Couldn't the whole world see that she was madly in love with him and nothing on earth would stop her becoming his wife and living with him for ever and ever?

She looked up at the high ceiling and saw a sparrow clinging to one of the rafters, probably waiting until everyone had gone away before making its escape into the spring sunshine. She knew how it must be feeling, cooped up in here when outside the primroses and daffodils were…

The entire congregation had gone terribly quiet. They were all waiting for her reply.

'I, Amanda Jane Grayson…' she began, in a clear, firm voice that seemed to echo up to the rafters where the inquisitive sparrow had now stopped chirping and appeared to be mesmerised by the ceremony below.

A barrage of cameras greeted them as they went out into the warm sunlight. Amanda found herself being kissed by relatives she remembered from her distant childhood but couldn't recognise or put a name to until prompted by her mother.

There were old school friends she hadn't seen for years, and a few of her friends and colleagues had travelled up from London. Alice, of course, had made the journey and was one of the first to congratulate them.

Yvonne, after having a couple of photographs taken with the bride and groom, had rushed away to breast-feed baby Caroline who was being cared for back at the house by one of Trevor's sisters, a retired trained nurse who was devoted to her new niece and had offered to help out when Yvonne was working.

Edward was holding tightly to her hand. 'Are you OK?' he whispered.

'I'll be fine when I can get out of this dress,' she whispered back, before putting on a bright smile for the cameras.

'I'll help you with the buttons.'

She giggled and another camera flashed. 'That's going to be a lopsided picture. Where's Tom?'

'Tom and Mark asked if they could take their jackets off, so I said of course they could. They're over in the field kicking a ball about with one of Trevor's sons.'

'But Tom hasn't had his photo taken with the bride and groom and…' She stopped, knowing that she was beginning to sound just like her mother. 'Oh, to heck with convention! He'll have lots of photos taken with us at Disneyland, won't he?'

Edward pulled her gently into his arms and gave her the spontaneous kiss that proved to be the best photograph in the wedding album. Little did either of them realise at the time that generations of Burrows were to stare at that photo and marvel that their ancestors could have been so romantic.

'Alone at last, to coin the cliché,' Edward said as Amanda snuggled against him in the guest room four-poster bed.

'Do you really like my wedding nightdress?' she asked, pointing to the white silk, thin-strapped garment suspended on a hanger from the top of the Queen Anne wardrobe. She'd spent ages choosing it and it had cost a fortune! Well, far more than she usually spent on such things.

'I told you; I really do like it.' He gave her a rakish grin. 'That's why I took it off you so that it wouldn't get creased or crumpled. But, to be honest, I prefer the feel of your skin and—'

'Edward!' She raised her head, brushing aside his lips before she became too involved and reality vanished. 'What time is our plane tomorrow?'

'Don't worry; it's all taken care of. The taxi arrives at eight. I'm going to waken Tom and Mark at seven and again every five minutes till they're up and dressed and cornflaked, so…'

She snuggled back into his arms. 'You're sure you don't mind taking Tom and Mark with us on our honeymoon? It's not very conventional, is it?'

He kissed the tip of her nose. 'Since when have we been conventional, either of us? It's going to work out perfectly. And we won't spend all our time in Disneyland, you know. We'll drift off to the beach—a little light sunbathing, some swimming, then back to the hotel for a siesta, whilst the boys join in with the hotel junior club. Not to mention the moonlit nights when we can lie in our room listening to the sound of the waves pounding on the shore…'

'It sounds wonderful! I'm glad we agreed to bring Mark as well. Those two boys are inseparable and it's been so good for Tom to have a surrogate brother whilst he's been growing up.'

Edward caressed the skin over her shoulders. 'It would be a good idea to give him a real brother or sister, don't you think?'

She smiled up into his eyes, feeling the urge to drown herself in the sensuous emotions that were welling up inside her as she capitulated to Edward's touch.

'You mean before Tom gets much older?' she murmured, moulding her body against his.

'The sooner the better, I would say…'

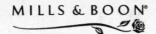

MILLS & BOON®

Makes any time special

**Enjoy a romantic novel from
Mills & Boon®**

Presents...™ *Enchanted*™ TEMPTATION.®

Historical Romance™ ⊬**MEDICAL
ROMANCE**™

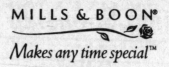

Coming Soon...

by
DEBBIE MACOMBER

Return to Promise to visit some old
friends...and meet some new ones.

Published 21st July 2000

Available this month from

MILLS & BOON®

⁀⅃ᴧ MEDICAL ROMANCE™

MOTHER TO BE by Lucy Clark

DOCTORS AT ODDS by Drusilla Douglas

A SECOND CHANCE AT LOVE by Laura MacDonald

HEART AT RISK by Helen Shelton

GREATER THAN RICHES by Jennifer Taylor

MARRY ME by Meredith Webber

Published 7th July 2000